Claimed by the Warrior

Claimed by the Warrior

A Pytheon Security Romance

Joss Wood

Claimed by the Warrior

Tule Publishing First Printing, December 2017

The Tule Publishing Group, LLC

ISBN: 978-1-948342-02-5

Chapter One

McKenna Dixon heard a thump in her hallway and the sound of heavy boots on her wooden floors. Daisy was too young and Leah, her nine o'clock client, too tiny to make so much noise. Besides, the front door was locked…wasn't it? After another heavy tread, McKenna walked to the half open door that separated her kitchen from the hallway and watched a six-foot-something example of pure, undiluted, prime grade male drop a very battered backpack on her highly polished wooden floor. He looked around her hall, dominated by an impressive, nineteenth century hand carved staircase.

He looked hot, he looked dangerous, he looked like someone she could imagine ripping off her panties and doing her up against the nearest wall. McKenna placed her fist on her sternum and sucked in what she prayed was a calming breath. *And this is why I should have regular sex, four or so years was far too long to go without having a proper, non-DIY orgasm. If I'd dated, had sex occasionally, I wouldn't be standing here, flushed and horny and wearing suddenly damp panties.* She'd tried to date, she argued back, and she now had a stalker who wouldn't leave her alone. Hasthtag EpicFail.

McKenna watched, fascinated, as he ripped his sunglasses

from his face, revealing deep set eyes under strong brows. Black designer cap, stubble, fascinating eyes with deep, gold irises ringed with black. Old, faded, clean, well-fitting jeans with a rip across a hard thigh and grubby, dusty tennis shoes. He yanked the cap from his head and ran his hands through his overlong, caramel-colored hair before shoving the ball cap into the back pocket of his jeans and hooking his glasses on the neck of his T-shirt. Seeing a clasp undone on the side pocket of his rucksack, he dropped to his haunches to fix it and McKenna noticed the long, well defined muscles bunching under his thin T-shirt, the curve of his buttock, the strength of his neck. She felt excited and unsettled and a little horrified that she was attracted to this messy, grumpy looking stranger. She didn't even know who he was…

McKenna yanked in a horrified breath. *God, she didn't know who he was!* She was just standing there like an idiot, perving over a strange man, and wondering how good his world class ass would feel under her hands and whether that mobile mouth could deliver the molten kisses she was fantasizing about.

She banged her palm against her temple to kick-start her brain. She had the brains of a flea; she wasn't 100 percent sure that her stalker was Craig; it wasn't like he'd signed any of his emails and the phone calls sounded like he was talking through a sock. So, in reality, her stalker could be anyone…*this could be him*! Or he could just be a handsome, ripped burglar. Or rapist. Or serial killer.

God, she had to stop watching those true crime channels.

Now spooked, McKenna heard light footsteps and she

closed her eyes in horror. She peeked through the open door and saw her little daughter skipping down the stairs, black curls bouncing and her smile as big as the sun. Her Rainbow nation child, with her milky, café au lait skin and light eyes, was a stunning mix of her Black Irish and Zoo's Malay and African ancestry.

"Hello, who are you?" she asked the sexy stranger, interested and curious. McKenna sighed. Daisy was anything but shy and retiring.

"Hello," he replied in a deep, mellow, sin-laced voice that sounded more English than American. "I'm Jed, who are you?"

"Daisy May Dixon," Daisy replied in her piping voice.

McKenna used the cover of her voice to ease the door open and, walking as quietly as she could into the hallway, reached for the baseball bat she kept hidden behind the large, potted ornamental lemon tree. Grabbing it, she lifted it to her shoulder.

"My mommy wants to hit you with a bat. What did you do to make her mad?" Daisy asked and McKenna released a heartfelt groan.

"Nothing yet but the day is still young." Sexy butt didn't turn around, didn't take his eyes off her daughter. "Can I ask you something?"

Daisy's brilliant blue eyes flashed with excitement. "Sure."

McKenna felt like an idiot just standing there, holding the bat up, not sure whether to swing or not. Neither the man nor Daisy seemed worried that she actually would take a swipe at his head. Huh.

He lowered his voice. "Is she still checking me out?"

"What do you mean?" Daisy asked, perplexed.

McKenna didn't give him the chance to explain. "I was not checking you out!" she stated, her voice hot and her face flaming. She lowered the bat and put one fist on her hip.

Sexy guy… Burglar…*the trespasser* slowly turned and sent her a cocky half-smile. "Yeah, you were. It's okay, I have no objection to hot women objectifying me."

"I was not…I…you…dammit!"

"Big people are weird," Daisy said on a heavy sigh as she continued her descent down the stairs. When she reached the bottom, she looked at McKenna. "Hitting people isn't nice, Mommy."

It was weird hearing her mommy-knows-best voice coming out of her daughter's mouth. McKenna swallowed a hot retort, but she kept a firm grip on the bat. She still didn't know who the guy was and her next appointment was Leah Hamilton, not this…*creature*!

"Sometimes it is."

McKenna glared at him. "Not helpful. Look, who are you and why are you in my house? How *did* you get in my house?"

He looked at the front door that stood open, allowing sunlight to spill into the hall. "Your front door was open and I walked on in. I thought this was a bridal salon?"

McKenna waved her hand toward a door opposite them. "The salon is through there. I work by appointment only and I don't have an appointment with you!"

His face tightened and McKenna caught the confusion that flashed in his eyes. She strengthened her grip on the bat and knew, with every atom in her body, that this man was dangerous. In more ways than ten.

He pinned her to the floor with those penetrating eyes. "I presume that you are McKenna Dixon?"

McKenna slowly nodded as Jed jammed his hands in the front pockets of those well-worn jeans.

Jed looked down at Daisy who, still staring up at him, was utterly fascinated. McKenna couldn't blame her; he was scrumptious to look at. Speaking of Daisy…she glanced at her watch. They were so late, again. This wasn't how she liked to start her day, especially when she had appointments with two of the pickiest socialites in Cape Town; one for a bridal gown and one for a ball gown. McKenna Dixon Designs. Who would've thought that the ex-party girl would make a reasonable living designing dresses?

"Mommy, when we get our puppies we're going to name them Dora and Boots," Daisy told her, sitting on the bottom stair and resting her chin in her hands.

"We're not getting puppies, Daisy." God, she couldn't do the puppy argument now. She didn't have the time or the inclination, especially since Daisy could teach mules a master class in stubbornness.

Daisy sent Jed a pleading look. "If I don't get a puppy I'm going to die."

Yeah, Daisy had definitely inherited Zoo's dramatic streak. She saw that sexy mouth twitch. He slowly nodded. "Then I definitely think that you should get a puppy."

McKenna banged the head of the bat on the floor.

"Still holding this, still prepared to use it," she quietly murmured.

Judging by his relaxed stance, he didn't look remotely concerned. She really had to work on her intimidation tactics.

McKenna glanced at her watch, realized how very late they were, and blew out a frustrated sigh. God, what a morning! And she still didn't know why she had a sexy man in her hallway at eight fifty a.m. McKenna turned at the sound of footsteps behind her and Mattie, her cousin and the seamstress who translated her designs from paper into actual dresses, walked into the hall from the kitchen.

"Late again?"

"Yep. I'm going to get another lecture from Mean Martha's African clone." McKenna shook her head. She was quite convinced the principal at Daisy's preschool waited at the gate to gripe at her for being late.

"Some things never change."

McKenna rolled her eyes, knowing that Mattie was referring to the hours she'd spent in the office of the lady principal of the exclusive, and pretentious, girls school they both attended back home in New York. She probably still held the record for being the most-suspended girl at St. C's. She'd been far too curious for school and her boredom had led to…incidents. Of course, her father—a rebel through and through—had thought that her antics were hysterical and only his hefty donations kept her in the exclusive school. God help her if Daisy's three-year-old mule-headedness translated into one iota of McKenna's rebellion. She'd been allowed to run wild, and she remembered how unsettling that was, so, with Mattie's help and encouragement, she'd decided to raise Daisy in as normal an environment as possible. That meant a mother who was consistently available, a modest house, chores, responsibilities. Everything she never had and needed most. McKenna closed her eyes and sent a prayer winging upward. *Dear Lord, I really don't want to raise myself.*

"You are the general's son," Mattie stated and McKenna was jerked back to the conversation. Mattie was holding out her hand to Jed, totally unfazed by his sex appeal or his hotty factor. Mattie was far too sensible to let his good-looks impact her. "You have his eyes."

"Yes, I'm Jed," he agreed. Judging by his thinning lips, he didn't seem happy with the comparison.

"Who is the gen'ral?" Daisy demanded, her puppy quest temporarily forgotten.

It was a fair question...if you were a child, McKenna conceded. But anyone with a lick of general knowledge about current affairs would know that Mattie was referring to Thaddius Hamilton, retired chairman of the Joint Chiefs of Staff at the White House and, thanks to his recent autobiography that was ruffling feathers back in the States, Simons Town's most famous part-time ex-pat. Jed's father had been pretty far up the US military and political tree. Jed was the living proof that one did get apples from orange trees since he was the most un-military looking man she'd ever seen.

Of course, if Jed was the general's oldest son then Leah

had to be…a bank bag of pennies dropped in McKenna's muddled-by-lust brain. Sexy Jed was Leah's brother and her intended man of honor. Admittedly, she'd only known him for about five seconds but she couldn't think of anyone less suited to the role.

Mattie looked around. "Where is Leah? Has she already gone through to the salon?"

Jed sent a narrow-eyed glance toward the front door to his right. "No, she hasn't arrived yet."

That was standard for Leah Hamilton. There was normal time and then there was Leah time.

Jed placed his hands on narrow hips. "Where the hell is she and why did I have to meet her here, at a bloody bridal salon? Dammit, I've been back in town for an hour and she's already driving me mad."

Daisy looked up at him and grinned. "Hell, dammit…" Daisy tested his words on her tongue.

"Daisy Dixon!" McKenna snapped her name out, ignoring the smile that appeared on Jed's face. It transformed him from good-looking to flat-out sexy and she desperately wanted to slap her mouth on his and find out what his smile tasted like.

Oh, God, she was in such deep trouble. She glared at him and Jed held up his hands in apology. "Sorry," he murmured but his amused expression didn't match his apology.

McKenna felt Mattie's hand on her shoulder. "I'll deal with this." McKenna sent her a grateful look. "Now, Miss Daisy, on the way to school we'll talk about what language is appropriate for a three-year-old."

"It's not fair! He said them first," Daisy muttered as she moved into the kitchen with Mattie.

Moving on to problem number two. McKenna looked at Jed; could Leah, minx that she was, really not have told her brother why they were meeting here, at her salon? McKenna pulled her bottom lip between her teeth and wondered how she could frame the next question without letting Leah's tiger-sized cat out of the bag. "Uh…what did she say when she asked you to meet her here?"

"She just gave me an address and told me to be here. That I shouldn't ask any questions and that she'd explain when she saw me."

Oh, crap, Leah hadn't told him a damn thing. That meant he didn't know about Leah's engagement and hell, no, she wasn't about to tell him. Leah could have that pleasure. Or, she looked at Jed's frowning face, that pain.

McKenna felt a headache gathering force at the back of her head and silently cursed when her mobile let out a couple of chirrups that stated she had a message. She didn't want to look; lately all the messages she'd received had been of the "I want to see you suffer" and "I want to show you what happens to women who think they are so damn special" variety.

She swallowed down the rush of fear and reminded herself to breathe. As much as she wanted to, she couldn't panic. Or let fear rule her. But, really, *what* had she done to attract this nutjob?

And speaking of nutjobs, she sent Jed a cool look. "You

can wait for your sister in the salon; she's normally never more than thirty or forty minutes late."

Jed narrowed his topaz-colored eyes. "Wonderful," he muttered.

"Aren't you going to read that?" he demanded when her mobile chirped again.

McKenna dug the phone out of the side pocket of her skirt and looked down at the number.

It wasn't a number she recognized and no, she didn't need to read it. It would be more of the same vitriol from her stalker and her morning had already been tough enough.

There was, she realized, only so much she could cope with in a thirty-minute time span.

★ ★ ★

JED WAS NORMALLY one of the fastest bullets on the firing range, but that wasn't the case today. He wished he could blame his fuzzy thinking on the fact that he hadn't had a proper night's sleep in far too long but that was a crock. He'd had the need for a solid eight trained out of him in the military.

No, the cause of his—temporary—confusion was walking across the hall, slim hips swaying. Black hair, gorgeous, green eyes, slender…stupidly attractive. She wore a fitted, scarlet, long-sleeved dress that ended above very pretty knees. Her calves were covered by knee-high, thin heeled leather boots and he wondered what she'd look like in a brief thong and those boots. Bloody sexy and his jeans instantly became one size smaller at the thought. Jed sighed. If he was getting semi-hard imagining this obviously uptight, dressed-so-appropriately woman naked then he definitely needed to find some action. Since he'd spent the last three months in a conservative Islamic country, willing women—and beer and song—hadn't been easy to come by. As a result, he'd been celibate for far too damn long and he was way overdue.

Waaay overdue. And while he had clocked her checking his ass—he was old enough and bad enough to recognize the corresponding attraction in those light, grape-green eyes—he was also old enough to ignore his enthusiastic dick and heed that warning siren, wailing from the far corner of his brain. *Bee-baw, trouble ahead.*

He'd, through trial and error, learned to listen to that blaring siren…

Stop watching her luscious ass and her swaying hips and get your head in the game, Hamilton! She stopped in front of the door to the salon and before she could turn the heavy knob, Jed moved in front of her, his flat hand pushing the door open so that she could precede him. He ignored her surprised expression and looked around the room. His skin prickled at what he saw. It was a large, utterly feminine room, with bay windows and pale walls and racks holding what looked like a million wedding dresses.

Suddenly spiders were crawling beneath his skin and his chest tightened.

"Coffee?"

Across the room, Jed noticed a rack holding corsets and garter belts and he was smacked in the head with a vision of

McKenna Dixon lying on the silver backless couch, breasts pushed up by that expensive lace and her legs spread, lacy, feminine garters encircling her slim thighs…

"Mr. Hamilton, would you like some coffee?"

It took all of his concentration to push that image away and to focus on McKenna's face. "Uh…no, I'm fine. Thanks."

McKenna looked uncertain and then shrugged. "As I said, you're welcome to wait but Leah might be a while."

Jed ran his hand across his forehead and felt the dots of sweat. Well, that was new…no matter what the circumstances he rarely, if ever, broke into a sweat. Maybe he was coming down with something.

Like wedding induced smallpox.

"I'll be back in fifteen minutes or so," McKenna told him and walked out of the room.

Jed just managed to swallow down the plea not to leave him alone in this version of hell.

MCKENNA DIXON LOVED her open plan kitchen and sitting room. She loved its cherry-red walls, its black-and-white harlequin floor, the fact that she could cook supper and watch Daisy in her play area, and sneak glances at the crime programs she loved on the flat screen on the far wall.

McKenna looked up when Mattie walked through the friends-and-family entrance, the kitchen door. Fifteen minutes had passed since Mattie had left to take Daisy to preschool and Leah had yet to arrive. She needed the restorative properties of coffee, stat. But coffee would have to wait because Mattie was carrying garment bags, which meant that she'd finished the sample dresses McKenna had designed and which would now complete her collection of vintage, new and designer gowns for the brides of Simons Town. McKenna clapped her hands in delight and reached for the zip of the dress bag which Mattie laid across the back of her black-and-white checked couch.

Mattie slapped her hands away. "Wash your hands first," she ordered.

McKenna did as she was told and, when she turned away from the sink to dry her hands, she saw Mattie standing over her computer, open on the granite kitchen counter, and that she was frowning. "He's *still* sending you emails?"

"Mattie, you can't just scroll through my inbox!"

"Why not? It's not like you have a life," Mattie retorted.

True. "He's still sending me text messages and calling me on the half hour between ten and one in the morning."

"No wonder you look like a raccoon," Mattie said. Mattie slapped her hands on her hips. "He's escalating. He started with a couple of emails begging you to give him another chance but—" she gestured to the screen "—these are nastier. How he'd like to get you alone, what he'd like to do to you…"

"Are you still convinced that the person doing this is Craig?" Mattie asked, tapping her fingernail on the edge of the laptop.

"Who else could it be?" McKenna dried her hands on a

kitchen towel. "Imagine how bad he'd be if we'd gone on more than two dates. Isn't it ironic that one of the blandest, most unassuming…slightly boring men I've met in a long time is a closet crazy?" Humor, she'd found, was a solid way to control the soul sucking fear.

"Only you." Mattie shook her head at her. "You are like a bad man magnet…if there's an unsuitable guy in fifty miles you'll end up dating him. It's a hell of a talent, my friend."

She didn't want to and she didn't mean to but she did exactly that, McKenna admitted. When she finally resolved to start dating again—she thought she'd like someone to share a meal with, some conversation, and, if she was really lucky, some sex—she'd decided to only accept dates from good, nice men. Men who were kind and pleasant and…*normal.* She wasn't looking for a relationship but on the off, off chance that she met someone who could change her mind—that notion had the same odds of Daisy receiving a much wished for unicorn for Christmas—then it would be with a reliable someone, someone who wouldn't let her down, who she wouldn't have to worry about. She'd dated enough of them—loved two of them—to be very convinced that bad, exciting, pulse jumping boys made terrible boyfriends. She had the experience to prove it.

She'd pulled bad boyfriend #1, Darren, from bar fights and bailed him out of jail; she'd loaned him money and her car. She'd caught him cheating. Yet her nineteen-year-old self had worshipped the ground he walked on and, admittedly, the sex had been brilliant. Then he'd fallen ill and instead of sticking around to help him through it, she bailed. He recovered, she—stupidly—begged him to take her back and he did. Full of remorse and still madly in love, she'd pandered to his every whim and he'd let her. Three months later, on the day of her twenty-first birthday, he dumped her by moving in with an eighteen-year-old tattoo artist with a daddy richer than hers.

Cue heartbreak.

A few years later, and another bad boy; this one was smarter and wilder and crazier than Darren and she'd fallen as hard and as fast. A couple of months of madness, too much champagne, and a broken condom led to Daisy's conception. Zoo had wanted her to have a quick abortion, blithely telling her she had to choose between him or the baby. She'd, not so blithely, chosen Daisy and, hours after she informed Zoo that she was going solo, he wrapped his Ferrari, and himself, around a tree.

Cue more heartbreak; deeper and harder and more vicious than before.

Nearly four years had passed since his death, and she still wasn't ready to risk having any type of a relationship with a man. Her two primary, adult relationships had been of the toss-tranquilizers down-her-throat variety and she didn't have the time or the energy to cope with another crazy, man related situation. Frankly, it was safer, and a great deal less messy—in every way possible—to go solo. And the fact that her one date since Zoo's death had turned out to be a stalker was, she believed, a big hint from the universe that dating was a bad idea and to stay far, far away from men.

And that definitely included Leah's hot brother…

She glanced down at the computer and the vitriol spouted there and her lips thinned in annoyance.

"I should report this to the police," McKenna said, closing the lid to her laptop.

"You can but there's little they can do. I checked." Mattie shrugged her shoulders. "The police force is small and they are already overworked. They won't be able to do anything since it's just emails and calls. Hopefully he'll get bored and stop soon."

"Hopefully." God, please. Anytime soon would be good. She didn't know how much longer she could keep putting on a brave face and she was thoroughly sick of constantly looking over her shoulder.

"On a happier note, take a look at the dresses," Mattie said impatiently, reaching past her to slide down the zip of the first garment bag.

McKenna gasped as she caught her first glimpse of the gorgeous, hand-beaded, ivory chiffon wedding dress. It was romantic and whimsical and her heart stuttered when she remembered that she'd designed this. She flung an arm around Mattie's shoulders and squeezed her to her side. "Oh, it's fantastic."

"That's the most detailed and intricate but the others are wonderful, too," Mattie said, reaching for another bag. They looked at the dresses and sighed some more before Mattie told her that she had two more dresses in her car.

"Go get them!" McKenna urged her. "I can't wait to see them. God, you are so talented, Mat. They are fantastic."

Mattie shrugged and efficiently zipped up the garment

bags. "I just sewed them together, I don't have the vision to design them."

"That's why we're a great team, we complement each other," McKenna told her as she walked away.

And Mattie was one of the reasons why she was still designing and selling wedding dresses as opposed to...well, raising llamas had at some point recently sounded like a fun thing to do. From the moment she announced her pregnancy, Mattie, though she was so very practical and sensible, had become her biggest cheerleader and helped her keep her eye on the ball.

She had enough money, Zoo's family insisted on paying maintenance for Daisy, and McKenna's father had left her a nice trust fund, but she'd soon realized that she couldn't keep chasing adventure, not with a baby in tow. Daisy needed stability, responsibility, consistency, for McKenna to finish what she started, as Mattie had insisted. McKenna still believed Daisy needed love above everything else, but she had listened to her cousin—nobody loved Daisy like McKenna did, but Mattie came a close second—and looked for a city she could settled down in. When Daisy was six months old, the three of them made the move to Cape Town, partly because she adored the city and also because Zoo's parents, siblings, and extended family called this city home. With both her parents dead and having no family she was close to—Mattie being the only exception—she wanted Daisy to grow up in the same city as her surviving grandparents and aunts and uncles and cousins whom she saw on a regular basis. And she adored this eclectic village on the east side of the Peninsular, not far from Cape Town itself, and she now had a proper home, a proper business and everyone was happy. Well, mostly. It was her little secret that she still, quite frequently, got itchy feet…

Itchy feet and curiosity and a sense of adventure…it was no shocker that was why she was, fatally, attracted to bad boys. They were interesting and exciting and usually too damn sexy for her to resist. But she was older and wiser now and she was going to give them, Jed Hamilton, and all men a very wide berth.

For sure.

The doorbell rang and McKenna sighed. Leah was only twenty-five minutes late she noticed as she picked up the sample dresses. Her time keeping skills were definitely improving.

Chapter Two

AFTER MCKENNA PULLED the door closed behind her, Jed dropped his pack to the floor and walked over to the bay window, shoving his hands into the front pockets of his jeans and looking out onto the busy street beyond the low, iron railing in front of her house. This part of Simons Town was an eclectic mix of residential and retail and McKenna Dixon's double story, narrow, blue-stoned house happily cohabited with the antique shops and art galleries, the book shop and the bakery. There was a coffee shop on the corner, so why weren't he and Leah meeting there, or at a diner? Why a bridal salon? Anyone who knew him—and he supposed that Leah didn't, not really—would know there was no earthly reason he'd get within ten feet of anyone selling anything wedding related. Intellectually he knew that marriage and babies weren't a contagious disease, but he wasn't prepared to take the chance.

He glared at the wedding dresses. He didn't do weddings; hell, his level of commitment was a couple of drinks and a one-night stand. And that wasn't because he was a dick—okay, *maybe* it was because he was a commitment phobic dick. That aside, he also had solid, practical reasons why he didn't do long-term relationships. He bounced around the world and was rarely in one place for longer than a week and, in his line of work, having a girlfriend or lover meant long periods apart and long-distance calls with terrible connections and hurriedly typed emails. And, yeah, too many hand jobs in the shower.

Besides, after being kicked in the emotional 'nads nearly a decade ago, he'd made a decision to keep his interactions with the nicer smelling sex light and fluffy and he had no intention of changing now.

Yet, here he was, in a freakin' bridal salon, cursing the fact that he had to meet his sister here, today, now…*urgently*. Frankly, he'd rather be back in the SWAT region, under fire from the Taliban, or sneaking into a drug lord's villa protected by Uzi-toting, trigger-happy psychopaths than be standing here.

Where he most wanted to be was back in Pakistan, looking for the eighteen-year-old son of the hotel magnate Neil Barker. Bo Barker was privately school educated, super bright, a golden boy extrovert who, according to everyone who knew him, had an incredible future ahead of him. The youngest son of moderate, liberal and philanthropic parents, no one thought he'd be radicalized by fundamental Islamists.

Turned out that nobody knew the kid at all because, despite his happy childhood and expensive education at one of the top boy's schools in the UK, Bo swiped one of his mom's credit cards and, girlfriend in hand, took a flight out of JFK to Islamabad. Hired by both sets of parents via Pytheon to find the runaways, Jed tracked them to their first hotel, then to the second. At the third hotel, the one they had yet to check out of, he exchanged a Ben Franklin for Bo's room number and, picking the lock, entered the shoe box room. Two rucksacks, bottles of water, a woman's hairbrush. A prayer mat facing east, his defiled passport and a battered copy of the Koran, with Bo's comments scribbled in the margins dispelled all suspicion that Bo had been kidnapped or coerced.

The rickety wooden chair was lying on its side, and Jax's rucksack—pink and purple—was slashed to ribbons. As were her clothes. Bo was exactly where he wanted to be. Jett didn't think Jax was…

His fears were confirmed a few minutes later. Pulling back the thin shower curtain, he'd found Jax, her naked body slumped over the rim of the tiny bathtub. Thanks to the swipe of an ultra-sharp, curved blade, her head remained attached to her neck by a couple of ligaments and her partially severed spinal cord. It was obvious that she'd been raped, in all ways possible by, probably, more than one man. She'd also been beaten beyond recognition. He identified her by the strands of her waist length hair not saturated by blood; they were the white blond described by both her parents and her passport description. The victim was also petite but the Snoopy Dog tattoo on the inside of her right ankle put her identity beyond doubt. Jax Petersen, eighteen and in love, suffered a horrible and brutal death.

The why wasn't so difficult to figure out. She was young blond, wearing the indecent and revealing clothing of jeans and a T-shirt in a country where men were not known for their liberated outlook on woman. That was one reason but another might be that the group Bo joined would've demanded a test of his loyalty and raping then killing his infidel girlfriend would be something they'd suggest.

Fucking bastards.

The police were called and after extensive questioning, and a call from Stone Smith, his big boss and owner of Pytheon International, to someone a lot higher up in the Pakistani Police Services than the captain who'd been interrogating him, Jett's handcuffs were removed. After another three hours of intense discussion, Captain Jat finally agreed that the most likely perpetrators were Jax's boyfriend and his new comrades. Jett's suspicions were confirmed when Stone, just last week, received a terse email from The Recruiter, with a nightmare inducing video attached. Jett watched Jax being raped, listened to that upper class plummy, English voice narrating the heinous act. Barker described how it felt to fuck her battered body, how easy it was to slit her throat…

Jett had discovered her body first and watched her die two weeks later. Both times, and every moment since, he vowed to track Bo down, to find him and bring him back to Islamabad, to hand him over to the Pakistani authorities so that his ass could be tossed into a shit hole jail where, as a blue eyed blond boy, he'd be extremely popular for a long, long time. And if something happened to him between tracking him down and capturing him—like, say, if Bo tried to fight his way out and gunfire was exchanged and whoops, look at that, rich, dead fucker—Jed wouldn't waste his tears.

But no, none of that happened. Despite his long stint in

Pakistan, the might of Pytheon International—a well-funded, highly covert, respected organization that routinely excelled in finding what was missing—behind him he did not manage to track Barker down. There were no sightings, no gossip, nothing suggesting that the British teenager was still in the city, or the country.

No matter how much money he offered, nobody opened their mouths which was strange in itself. Money usually made people talk. The amount he'd been flashing should've made somebody sing like a frickin' canary. But he'd gathered precisely…shit.

After three excruciatingly frustrating months Seth, his boss and commanding officer ordered him home. Whether home was his apartment in New York City or Cape Town, they didn't care. They just wanted him and his simmering temper out of Pakistan.

Despite having failed Jax and her parents, he'd had no choice but to leave. He'd run out of avenues to explore, sources to tap. He was attracting attention, attention neither he nor Pytheon wanted or needed. Certain people were starting to suspect that the photo-journalist who was outraged at the death of his fellow Brit, might be more than what he portrayed himself to be. It had been time to exit but leaving without being able to find Jax's killer burned numerous holes in his stomach.

Intellectually, he knew he needed distance, some time to decompress, to get Jax and her fate out of his head. Emotionally, he wanted nothing more than to string Barker up by his balls and with him, the piece of shit who recruiting these kids down this path to hell. He didn't understand any of this…why did a supposedly normal kid leave his upper class lifestyle to become a radicalized freedom fighter, flipping his life upside down to fight for a cause that was so very and, yeah, fundamentally different from everything he knew?

The answer lay in whoever, or whatever "The Recruiter" was. While Jed tracked Bo's whereabouts, Seth and Cracker, back at Pytheon headquarters were cyber-tracking The Recruiter, a mysterious figure who was recruiting young people into cults, organizations and religions for money.

Cracker, Pytheon's shit-hot white hacker, had found connections between The Recruiter and Bo Barker. The Recruiter had been Barker's entrée into a world of fundamentalism and radicalization and, apparently, rape and murder. Jed felt his blood pressure rising and deliberately dropped his shoulders, sucked in a few cleansing breaths of sweet smelling air. He was in Cape Town, on a forced vacation, he'd might as well relax, as much as he could. Looking out of the window, Jed watched a couple walk past the house; he wore a pair of battered board shorts that hung low on his hips and matted dreadlocks that reached his waist. His companion was dressed in full black, jeans, a long-sleeved T-shirt and she had a fine silver chain looping from her eyebrow to her lip. Both were barefoot. Cape Town, arty, vibey, alternative. Funny how his half-American, half-English family had adopted this most southern, and most beautiful, city on the African continent as their home town. He supposed it wouldn't have happened if his English grandparents hadn't retired here, if he and then, much later,

Leah hadn't spent their summer holidays with them. After his mom died, Leah decided to move to Cape Town to be closer to the grandparents and never bothered to move back to the States. Leah's career in real estate led to the general and his new child-bride purchasing a holiday home here when Thaddius retired a few years back. Jed hadn't escaped Leah's attention either, and she nagged him into buying a penthouse apartment with a spectacular view of False Bay and the endless, wild, rollicking coastline.

"Big brother!"

He turned and there she was, standing in the doorway, all five feet of utter femininity, dressed in a multi colored sundress that ended too far above her knees, ridiculously big sunglasses that covered most of her face and a smile that had all the power of a nuclear explosion. Leah, his baby, younger-by-twelve-years, sister. And, thanks to the age gap between them, a virtual stranger. His mom would've hated that…

Jed ignored that thought and winced as she ran toward him on stupidly high heels. In order to keep her from breaking her neck, he moved quickly and within a couple of strides swept her off her feet and into his arms. He heard her gurgle of laughter as he easily lifted her off her feet to drop a kiss onto her smiling lips. "Hey, shrimp."

"You're here, you're really here." Leah wrapped her arms around his neck and buried her face into his neck. "I can't believe that you're finally back home!"

Well, home was a relative term. Jed lowered her to her feet and plucked her sunglasses off her face, startled to see tears brimming in her bright blue eyes. "It hasn't been that long, Leah."

Leah's tiny hand smacked his chest. "It's been more than a year, Jed! A year!"

Jed frowned. That long? Could it be? He'd slipped home in between assignments last year... doing an underwater shoot of a shipwreck in the Caribbean and then tracking and photographing the desert lions in Namibia. On a yacht near the reef, he'd found the Manet that had been stolen from a small art gallery in the Netherlands and in Namibia he'd picked up a trail of a multi-national gang who were dealing in blood diamonds. The last three months had been dedicated to finding Barker and Jax's killers, so yeah...a year could've passed.

Leah stepped away from him and her thin brows lifted as she gave him a long up and down and up again look. "Dear God, you look like a...backpacker. Like you haven't slept in a week."

Jed looked at his reflection in one of the three floor to ceiling mirrors behind her. He'd admit he wasn't looking his best. He had showered at the airport—first class rocked—and changed his T-shirt, but he still looked like he'd been pulled through a bush backward.

"I had this idea of heading straight to my place and sleeping for eight straight but my bossy, little sister insisted that I meet her...now, today. No excuses, I was told in a certain snotty email, would be tolerated."

Leah waved his words away. "Then you should've made your earlier flight. You were supposed to be here days ago! Seriously, how long can it take to shoot a couple of photographs?"

Jed shrugged and, as was his habit, didn't give an explanation. What could he say? *I've been looking for a rich teenager who found a new, messed up version of a perfectly peaceful religion and, to fight for his new cause, pulled his girlfriend into a strange country, handed her over to be raped and tortured before slitting her throat?*

Yeah, no.

How wonderful it would be to live in Leah's wonderful, uncomplicated, danger free world.

"That's really no excuse for looking like an itinerant traveler, Jed," Leah gently chastised him. "I know you have *some* money. Surely you can afford some better clothes."

Yeah, he had "some" money. He had invested in property around the world and had a bank account that would make even his snobby sister blink twice. He recovered people and property that were, occasionally, priceless, and the clients, via Pytheon, paid him a very hefty commission when he succeeded, which he always did. And the money he earned from his photographs wasn't too shabby either.

As for his clothes, he didn't need to wear thousand dollar suits and shiny shoes to make him feel like a million bucks. In the world he operated in, both the journalistic and the dangerous, his clients only cared about results; he could look like a three-headed toad and they wouldn't give a crap. Besides, with Leah's chatty mouth, there was always a chance that the general would hear that Jed wasn't living up to the illustrious Hamilton name. It wasn't mature, but irritating his father was still one of his favorite hobbies.

He glanced at the rack of wedding dresses and then back down into his little sister's face. "So, shrimp, want to tell me why we are meeting in a bridal salon?"

"You haven't worked it out yet?" Leah nibbled the edge of her plump lower lip as she started to walk toward dresses, flipping through them at speed. "Well, I'm getting married and I want you help me choose my bridal gown. It's your first job as my man of honor."

Jed resisted the urge to pound the ball of his hand against his ear. He felt like an IED had just exploded under his feet and he felt shaky and disorientated. Jesus, had she really said that she was getting married and—*what?*—that she wanted him to be her man of honor, whatever the hell that was?

"I didn't know that you were dating anyone!" Jed muttered. "And that was something that *could* be shared in an email, dammit!"

"It happened quite fast," Leah replied. "We want to get married as soon as we can."

Not. Gonna. Happen.

No way. No how.

Jed shook his head, irritated that his breathing felt irregular, that his heart was pounding a thousand beats per minute. Leah married? He didn't think so! She was still a baby, barely twenty-four. And who was she marrying and what the hell did a "man of honor" do? It didn't matter because none of this was happening…he didn't care if the general, or God, had given her permission to do this. He was her older brother and *thiswasn'thappening*! The general had the parental skills of a potted plant so his permission meant jack shit. No, until he'd met Leah's fiancé and run a deep background check on him and put him through a couple of paces, there was no way Leah was getting hitched.

No way, no *bloody* how.

His decision made, Jed shook his head and straightened his spine. He was ex-SAS and was now a kick-ass recovery agent. He'd been in some of the stickiest and dangerous situations in the world. This shouldn't even be a blip on his radar but…

Dear hell-holes and crappy regions of the world, he thought as McKenna Dixon walked into the room, *all is forgiven*.

McKenna greeted Leah Hamilton with a kiss on her cheek and a brief hug. Resting her hands on her shoulders, McKenna gave her an assessing look. Beneath her expertly applied makeup McKenna could see the blue stripes under her eyes that suggested that she hadn't been sleeping, and her normally quick-to-smile mouth looked pinched and drawn. "Are you okay, honey?" she quietly asked.

"Been better," Leah whispered back. "Jed is less than enthralled about being my man of honor."

"I'm even less thrilled about you getting married." Jed's deep voice traveled across the room toward them. "Who is this guy? What does he do? Why not wait? *Why is this the first time I am hearing about this?*"

Leah stepped away from McKenna and placed her hands on her slim hips. "When exactly could you have met him,

Jed? You haven't been home in over a year! Whenever I call, you can't talk because you're in some godforsaken area with spotty cell signal and this wasn't something I wanted to tell you via email. I can't just put my life on hold until you have some time for me!"

McKenna was watching Jed's hard face and she caught a wisp of emotion cross his eyes…pain? Regret? A combination of both? Whatever she saw was gone in the next blink of his eyes and they, and his face, were once again unreadable. McKenna pushed her hair out of her eyes and looked at him, leaning a thick shoulder into her pale wall. She'd had men in this space before, men who accompanied their fiancées or daughters on their quest to find the perfect dress, but nobody had dominated this space like Jed was currently doing. His body, obviously in prime condition—dear Lord, she'd love to see him naked—radiated masculinity and strength, but the rare flash of a roiling emotional volcano beneath that calm, cool, composed façade fascinated her.

He was the trigger to why she'd been musing about her previous lovers earlier. In her old life as crazy girl, she'd met a bad boy or two, but they were pale imitations of the real thing…the real thing being that six-foot something combination of danger, power, and take no prisoners attitude. He was it, a bad boy alpha male, the biggest, baddest dog in the junkyard. And, naturally, he excited the hell out of her.

Bad, bad, terrible idea! You're not doing bad boys anymore, remember? You are a jerk magnet, attracted to the weird and crazies of the world. And hadn't the point been hammered home recently? You thought that you'd found a guy who was normal, and nice, and had potential and he turned out to be a raving, obsessive lunatic.

Self-love had to be the answer, she decided. Not as much fun but infinitely safer.

"Has the general even met this dude who thinks he is going to marry you?" Jed's question broke into her thoughts.

McKenna took a step back and sighed. Obviously there wasn't going to be any talk about dresses until these two worked their issues out. Maybe she should leave them alone…

"Of course he's met Heath." Leah snapped back as she took a seat on one of the low, backless benches that faced a bank of mirrors and a dais. "He likes him, I love him, and I am going to marry him, with your approval or not." Leah pulled out a tablet from her bag and sent her brother a long, cool look. "I am going to discuss wedding dresses with McKenna now so you can either stand there looking like a thunder cloud or you can get with the program and give me your input. Your choice. But either way, get out of my face."

Jed jerked back and McKenna grinned at the shocked expression on his face, sure that it was the first time his sister, hell, probably any woman, had talked back to him. She was certain he was more used to members of her species hanging off his every word, drooling, and begging him to scratch their tummies. Or other, more interesting parts of their anatomy.

Good for you, Leah, she silently cheered her on. The man needs to be taken down a peg or three hundred.

"I haven't had enough sleep for this," Jed muttered as he

walked over to the couch, rubbing his sexy stubble. He sent Leah a dark look but negated the effect by drifting his tanned hand over Leah's blond head. He slumped down next to Leah and stretched out his long legs. "Can I at least meet Mr. Wonderful before you say 'I do'?"

Leah narrowed her eyes at him. "Maybe. If you agree to leave your weapons at home."

Jed's attempt to look innocent was laughable. "What weapons?"

"The H&K that's behind your back and the Smith that's strapped to your ankle," Leah retorted, not giving him an inch.

Jed sat forward and lifted his shirt up and revealed the tanned strip of his back above the waistband of his jeans. It was smooth and muscled and gun free. And hot. So hot.

Hand me a fan, the temperature inside the salon was skyrocketing and it had nothing to do with weather.

"Not packing, honey."

Not guns anyway. McKenna resisted the urge to fan her face.

"Good, keep it that way," Leah told him. "Guns make Heath nervous."

Jed looked up at the ceiling and McKenna saw his throat bob in an effort to hold down a retort. Maybe there was hope for the man.

Then Jed leaned sideways and stared down at Leah's tablet screen. Standing behind them, she looked past their heads to the picture that appeared on the screen. It was a cream puff dress, with tiers of ruffles, over the top beading and a shape that would swallow up Leah's petite frame. Leah traced the picture with her fingernail and McKenna could see that she genuinely loved the dress.

"Dang, that's ug-lee!" Jed stated.

Man of honor? McKenna rolled her eyes. "Moron" of honor was a far better description.

Chapter Three

McKenna, a headache pounding at the base of her skull, gave Leah a final hug and sent a thank-you-God that their first session was finally over. Leah, bless her, had tried on at least twenty of the sample gowns she kept in the small room adjacent to the salon—her designs and from other designers she worked with—and she'd hated them all. They couldn't even decide on a shape she preferred: mermaid, princess, sheath, sexy. Or a color. Pure white, ivory, color-tinted...Leah was the pickiest bride McKenna had ever encountered.

And it didn't help that every time she asked for her opinion, Leah glanced at Jed before she answered. It was as if she wanted his approval before committing herself to anything and he'd given her absolutely nothing. His one and only comment he'd uttered had been on the first dress they'd looked at on the tablet and since then he'd been as silent as a painted monk. He'd just watched as Leah modeled one dress after another and McKenna was convinced that Leah was indecisive because she so desperately wanted a reaction from her brother, she wanted his involvement and that she wouldn't give up until she got it. If that meant trying on a hundred dresses then that was what she would do...

And Jed wouldn't budge because any involvement in the process would be tantamount to his giving his approval and that wasn't going to happen either.

McKenna didn't have time for the games the Hamilton siblings were playing and had no wish to get caught up in their drama as she was dealing with enough of her own. But Leah was her client and she was the person she needed to keep happy. The brother? Not so much. She needed to get a couple of things straightened out with him and pronto...she was not prepared to deal with a picky bride for the next few months.

On her way out of the salon, Leah lifted her mobile to her ear and was quickly absorbed into a conversation, so McKenna placed her hand on Jed's forearm to keep him from following his sister out of the room. Underneath her fingertips, she could feel the raised veins, the texture of the light sprinkling of arm hair, the warmth of his skin.

Lust, lust, go away...don't come back another day. Concentrate, Dixon!

"We need to talk." McKenna yanked her hand away and walked around him to shut the door to the hallway.

Jed lifted one dark brow as she placed her hands behind her back and thought about what it was, exactly, that she wanted to say. *You have the sexiest lips ever? What would they feel like on mine? God, McKenna, get a grip.* She hauled in a breath.

"I don't want you accompanying Leah here anymore."

Jed just looked at her and lifted his shoulder in a small shrug. "It's not my idea of a fun time either." He rubbed the back of his neck. "The last place I want to be after three months of being woken up by a muezzin, calling people to prayer at the ass-crack of dawn, is in a froufrou bridal salon watching my sister playing wedding day Barbie."

McKenna wanted to ask him where he'd been, but his don't-ask expression kept her words behind her teeth. "My salon is not froufrou."

"It still has wedding dresses in it," Jed snapped back. He walked away from the couches to the window and looked out onto the busy street. The area was a curious mixture of houses and businesses, some—like her building—a mixture of both. It was a hippy but upmarket area of town with artists and sculptors and antique dealers mixing happily. She and Daisy were happy here.

"Have you met him?"

"Leah's fiancé?"

His sharp nod was his only response. McKenna took a moment, wondering what to say. She had met Heath when she'd attended an exhibition at the art gallery down the road. She'd liked him; he seemed to be kind, sensitive, maybe a little nerdy with his rangy body and floppy hair and his horn-rimmed glasses. Pretty normal, all in all, but she remembered thinking that there were hidden depths to Leah's guy. It wasn't anything she could put her finger on, she couldn't explain it, but there was something more to Heath than the mild mannered computer geek Leah introduced him as. "I liked him."

Unsurprisingly, Jed wasn't reassured. "She's too young to be getting married," he growled.

"There isn't a right or wrong age to get married," McKenna retorted, "just the wrong person you choose to marry. And you can make the wrong choice as well at eighty as you can at eighteen."

"Is that the voice of experience I hear talking?"

McKenna frowned at him and ignored his question. Like she was going to share her traumatic, soap opera past with a guy she'd met an hour ago. "Getting back to my point, please don't come accompany Leah here again. She wants your approval, your input, and not getting that from you makes the entire process a lot more difficult than it has to be."

And you distract me, big time. And the last thing I need right now is to be distracted by a hunky man with shadows in his eyes.

"Getting back to *my* point..." Jed folded his arms across his chest and his eyes slammed into hers. "Single, married, divorced?"

She widened her eyes, aiming to look innocent. "All at the same time? That must keep you busy."

"Haha, funny. You know that I am asking about you. What's the story with Daisy's father?"

"That's none of your business," McKenna quietly stated.

Jed just looked at her, saying nothing, his expression demanding a response.

McKenna considered challenging him to a staring competition but knew that she didn't have a hope of winning so she shrugged. "Why do you want to know?"

"Because we could start a wildfire from the sparks bouncing between us," Jed prosaically replied. "So, what is it?"

"I am a single mother and planning to stay that way." She lifted her hand as a satisfied expression crossed his face. That admission meant he was now the predator and she was the prey. Not a situation she felt comfortable with.

"It's not going to happen, Slick," she said, knowing that she wouldn't have to paint him a picture for him to understand her cryptic statement.

"Oh, yeah, it so is," Jed assured her, his eyes on her mouth.

"It's really not."

"You have an objection to hot sex?"

Not in general, no, but she did have a massive problem with how much she wanted it from him. Not that he needed to know that, ever. "I *object* to the fact that you think that, with a snap of your fingers, I'll fall into bed with you, incredibly grateful for your attention," McKenna said, her voice credibly cool. "It's not going to happen, I promise you."

The corners of Jed's mouth tipped up and his eyes lightened to the color of old gold. "What if you snap your fingers and I feel incredibly grateful for your attention? Which I would be."

He stopped when they were an inch apart and she could feel his breath caressing her temple. His fingertips skimmed her side before his hand settled on her hip. It took everything she had not to close that gap between them, to push her tight nipples into his hard chest, to align her hips with his. She wanted him but she didn't want to want him...bad boys, demanding alpha men were so not her style.

Well, not anymore. She'd learned her lesson.

"And you *promise* me?" Jed's voice was low but dangerous in her ear as his hand moved up from her hip to the back of her neck. His fingers held her in a rock solid grip and McKenna felt like her heart had been attached to a rocket. "Honey, your mouth shouldn't write checks your ass can't cash."

"What—?"

He cut the word off when his mouth slammed on hers. His other hand wrapped around her hips and he pulled her up against the long, hard length of him and, dear Lord, he was long and hard, *everywhere*. McKenna's mind flitted from sensation to sensation, unable to decide what thrilled her the most. His clever mouth and slick tongue, swiping hers, demanding that she come out and play? His broad hand, one flattened between her shoulder blades and the other cupping her butt, keeping her pressed up close and personal against his so-hard cock? The smooth skin of his lower back that her hands discovered beneath his loose T-shirt?

It was all too much, he was too much. Too fast, too hard, too masculine and, within a heartbeat, that all changed. As if he was tuned in to her, Jed gentled his touch, pulling back slightly. His mouth geared down from crazy hot to a soft warm as his hands moved up to her face, his fingertips tracing the line of her jaw, feathering over the arches of her cheekbones. The kiss softened even more to nips and licks and he then he lifted his mouth and moved his hands to her shoulders.

Yet his eyes, the same color as Roman gold—and as old—remained locked on hers. She tasted him on her bottom lip and rocked on her heels. What was there to say when you'd shared something wildly elemental, something unexplainable?

"Jed! Let's go!"

Jed's eyebrow lifted at Leah's demanding holler. As he placed more distance between them, McKenna noticed that his erection had disappeared and he looked like he had before; calm, inscrutable, composed. Where did he put all that heat she'd felt in his kiss? She couldn't resist flicking a glance at her reflection in the closest mirror. Wild eyes, mussed hair, flushed skin…

Jed looked unperturbed, as if kissing the hell out of a woman was part of his daily routine, and she looked like she'd surfed the bands of a whirlwind. And that, McKenna decided as her mind trundled up to its normal processing power, was why she couldn't play this game anymore.

She had the quick and crazy and she'd had her fair share of relationships that flamed furiously and died as quickly. And to carry on with the fire metaphor, two that flamed furiously and ended her heart being tossed into an inferno. Besides, if she wanted some hot sex, she wanted to share the experience with someone who rated it a bit higher than, say, ordering coffee or doing laundry. She didn't require love or a happily ever after but it had to be more than a quick, hard, physical release. She could do that on her own, or with Mr. Happy. *Thank you very much.*

"So, when can I see you again?" Jed demanded, sending a

quick glance towards the still closed door.

McKenna shook her head. "Still not happening, Slick."

"Why the hell not?" Jed's eyes narrowed in annoyance.

The door knob started to turn and she quickly flung her words at his head. "I have a toy, thanks, and it does the job you're offering quite well. It's fast, it's efficient and best of all, it doesn't talk!" McKenna slapped a hand on his chest and sent him a cool glance. "Don't come back to my salon again."

"Oh, I'll be back," Jed promised her, his voice low and laden with promise. He bent his knees so that his eyes were level with hers. "And, Legs, sex shouldn't be fast and efficient. It should be slow and sexy and messy and hot. With lots of talk. I'm going to show you just how it's supposed to be."

"Arrogant, macho bullshit," McKenna muttered to his departing back. But she, stupid as she was, couldn't help feeling excited at the prospect of Jed doing just that.

JED SHOVED HIS mobile into the pocket of his running shorts and picked up his pace, his feet slapping the sidewalk as he passed the double and triple story mansions that made up this part of Simons Town. It was getting harder to manage his two careers, he thought, reflecting on the conversation he'd just ended with the features editor at *Go West*. He had agreed with Pytheon when they'd chosen photography to be his cover story; it had always been a passion of his and he genuinely enjoyed the challenge of capturing the essence of the subject or situation in far flung places. His subsequent press accreditation and affiliation with one of the most iconic and well respected magazines in the world gave him access into places that normal tourists would never see and audiences with people who were generally inaccessible. That access was invaluable to him as a recovery agent.

The problem was that he was becoming a little too well-known, far too conspicuous. His photographs were garnering awards and he was starting to find it difficult to fly under the radar as well as he used to. In the early days, he was just another grunt trying to make a living with his Nikon but now his name attracted attention. Attention was something that undercover recovery agents tried to avoid.

On the other hand, photography—and his success at it—made the general gnash his teeth and that had to be a good thing. A few years back he had been, probably, the only man in the country, apart from the president, who didn't call his father "sir." Then again, nobody but he and Leah had the dubious honor of calling the general "Dad." Jed sighed, thinking of his childhood as a child soldier in Thaddeus Thomas Hamilton's private army. His father had controled, pressured and frustrated all of them with his constant pursuit of perfection; when it came to his family and how it was perceived there were no shades of imperfect gray. He'd always longed for freedom and independence but he knew that if he did his mother, and sister, would also pay the price for his rebellion. Nobody could hold a grudge like the general.

After school, doing something other than joining the military would've been a perfect "screw you" but, despite his father, Jed had wanted, desperately, to serve. Not because it was what Hamiltons did, because it was expected of him, but because he'd loved the idea of the military; it had always been what he wanted to do.

He was exceptionally lucky that he had two countries he could call home—thanks to his mother, he had dual-citizenship—and instead of joining the Army Rangers, as his father had expected him to, he'd enlisted in the British Army and had moved on to the elite British Special Air Service instead. His father had blown a gasket or two and the commendations he received hadn't mollified him in the least. By the way the general acted anyone would think that he'd joined the Taliban. As a result, his father never acknowledged or discussed Jed's army career or acknowledged or even spoke to him.

Win.

Then his world properly flipped over when his mother was diagnosed with cancer when he was in is mid-twenties. Unable to return home for six weeks after he received the news, he'd been shocked at the frail, thin, weak…lonely… bedbound woman when he had. His father, Jed found out, had hired 'round the clock nurses but hadn't, according to those excellent women, visited his mom for three weeks. Before he could make an appointment to see his father—there was a crisis somewhere in the world that needed his attention—his mom passed on. Four months later the general married a woman three years younger than his oldest child.

It didn't take much digging to realize that the general had been having an affair for two years prior to his mom's death. Finding out about his infidelity, and that the general had a "do as I say but not as I do" policy had been Jed's personal tipping point. Alone, a little lost, a lot bereaved, and questioning his life and his choices, he left his unit and then the UK with nothing more than his Nikon and a backpack. Six months later, Pytheon found him and under the cover of working as a freelance photographer, he used his combat skills to right wrongs.

Jed felt the vibration of his mobile in the inside pocket of his running shorts and abruptly stopped. Removing the phone, he lifted the small, but powerful, device to squint at the screen. Seth…crap. If Jed believed in having a boss, and he didn't, then Seth would be the closest person fitting the description. He was also, Jed reluctantly admitted, a curious mixture of brother, cousin, friend, and drinking partner. Annoyingly, Seth was also the only person he'd ever come across who could kick his ass in hand-to-hand combat. *That had to change.* Jed scowled. No office bound, pencil pusher should be able to do that.

"What?" he demanded after answering the call. The faint buzz on the line reminded him that they were using one of the most highly encrypted lines in the world.

"Where are you?"

Jed's teeth snapped together. "You have satellite tracking on my phone; you know damn well that I landed yesterday and that I'm in Cape Town."

"Simons Town, to be precise. Coastal town, home to the main naval base. Victorian buildings, quaint streets and walkways and is situated between the mountains and the beach."

"Thank you, Google."

Seth ignored his sarcasm. "And yesterday you spent part of the morning in a bridal salon?"

Jed briefly considered lobbing his mobile into the sea but there were other tracking devices that Seth used. In Jed's watch, his wallet, belts. It was standard operating procedure for Pytheon operatives. They were the best of the best and Pytheon didn't like losing any of them.

"Could you pick up that hives were breaking out all over my body?" Jed grumbled.

Seth started to whistle *"Here Comes the Bride."*

"Screw you," Jed told him. "I'd rather face a firing squad."

Seth just whistled louder and Jed lifted his eyes to the bright African sky, knowing that Seth was baiting him. "What do you want, Halcott? Please tell me that you called because you have an assignment for me."

Seth snorted in his ear. "What part of mandatory leave did you not understand, Jed? You need this downtime and if I could stop you from taking assignments from that magazine I would do that too."

"That magazine" was the most iconic publication in the world dedicated to documenting exploration, adventure, and different cultures of the world. He looked around to make sure that no one could hear his next statement before speaking again. "My work as a photojournalist is an excellent cover," Jed said, his voice mild even though he could feel a vein pounding in his temple. "And I don't need a break. Not from the magazine or from my duties to Pytheon."

Seth snorted. "Well, I happen to disagree. Your recent psych evaluation suggested that you need some time to decompress, to unwind. You've been on back-to-back assignments for nearly a year and we think you are flirting with burnout. Here, at Pytheon, we like our people to be firing on all cylinders, all the time."

What a crock. He was *fine* but nobody would bloody believe him. And Seth, apparently, did have the power to put him on mandatory leave. *Bastard.*

"You need a break, Jed, and I'm insisting that you take one. Besides, since your face is on the cover of one of the most popular magazines in the world this month, you're a bit too recognisable at the moment."

Jed pulled a face. He ran his hand over his four-day beard, still frustrated that he couldn't talk the editors out of *not* using the picture.

"Admittedly, it's been a year or two since I was in the field, but I would think that the premise of 'keeping a low profile' would still be advantageous when you liberate people, documents, jewels, art, and secrets," Seth stated and Jed heard the irritation in his voice.

Since Seth was frequently annoyed with him—Jed broke too many rules and took too many unnecessary risks for Seth's peace of mind—Jed didn't worry about it.

He preferred the description "recovery agent" but Seth

was right. On behalf of many Western governments and her allies, her business people, and their friends, he "liberated" items that had been stolen from them. And he got paid very well to do that. And having his face on the cover of the best-selling magazine in the world was seriously counterproductive.

He'd apologize but that, as his father and the military had drummed into him was—along with being emotional—a sign of weakness. Not his thing.

So he changed the subject. "The magazine has offered me an assignment to do a photo shoot of Venezuela, documenting the country's unrest. I'm considering taking the job and want to head to Caracas in a week or so. So, do you have anything that's bubbling down there?"

"Nice try but your mandatory leave is for a month at the minimum. Anyway, I don't currently have any situations down there that complies with your conditions."

Dammit. When he'd joined Pytheon, he'd quickly realized that sometimes Pytheon took on certain assignments so that their biggest client could claim plausible deniability when an undesirable "element" was removed from society. He'd made it very clear early on that he wasn't available for those assignments. He broke rules on a regular basis but taking a life would tip him over the edge of the abyss he routinely danced on. The devil had his sticky paws on his soul once or twice, but it was still mostly his.

He planned on keeping it that way for as long as he could.

"I also called to tell you that we received another email

from our favorite fuck head," Seth calmly stated. But underneath the calm was roiling anger.

Every muscle in Jed's body tensed. "And?"

Dear God, he didn't think he could watch another video of Jax's death. The last one had him making offers to the god of the porcelain bowl. "It was a series of photos of Barker undergoing training in bomb making and firearms, at some unidentified training camp. We couldn't identify his comrades, they were all masked but Barker is front and center, long blond beard, very blue eyes. Unmistakable."

"So what was the point of sending those images them to us?"

Seth was quiet for half a minute. "We can't work that out. According to Sam, it feels like The Recruiter is taunting us, even daring us to find him."

"Why bother? Isn't he supposed to recruit, get paid, shut the hell up?"

"Sam seems to think that we've pissed on his batteries somewhere along the line, that he's taking pleasure in showing that he's smarter than us."

Sam was Stone Smith's sister, held a PhD in criminal psychology and was an expert in deviant behavior. The slim redhead specialized in serial killers and frequently consulted with Pytheon International. She was both brainy and sexy, a hell of a combination. She was also the man-who-paid-his-salary's sister and Jed believed in not dating where he worked.

Jed's hand curled around his mobile, white knuckling the device. "Let me come back, Seth. I'm good to go."

It was a measure of how much this case worried him that Seth took so long to answer. "I really believe that you need the break, Jed, but if something happens, if something breaks, I'll pull you back so fast your head will spin." Before he could offer another argument, Seth spoke again, his tone clearly stating that the subject was closed. "Anyway, get some rest, lie on the beach, get laid," Seth told him.

He had better things to do, like track down that scumbag, Barker. Jed ground his molars together. "Is that an order?"

"Like you take orders," Seth snorted. "Consider it a strong suggestion," he added before hanging up.

Strong suggestion, his ass. Jed slowed his pace and looked around to get his bearings. He'd run further than he'd expected and was now heading toward McKenna's house. Talk about being led by his dick.

McKenna was freaking fascinating, he admitted. The kiss they'd shared…okay, he knew that he'd gone without sex for a while but he'd never, even when he broke his driest of dry spells, come close to losing control like he had with her. He never lost control, period. He'd learned the lesson early and he'd learned the lesson hard; his father exploited any weakness demonstrated and losing control—of his temper, of his mouth, of his expressions—would be to his disadvantage. And as an adult, the one time he'd felt safe enough to express his fears, he'd been kicked in the gut. As a result he avoided attachment, kept himself composed physically and emotionally distant and he always, always maintained a tight rein over his control.

So what the friggin' hell had happened when he kissed her?

He'd gone longer without a woman, without sex, without having such a combustible reaction, so why with this woman and why now? He'd had plenty of gorgeous women and hadn't felt half as much. With one, deep kiss it felt like McKenna had pushed her hand into his chest cavity, found his heart, and squeezed.

This was a surprise since he thought that he'd lost all feeling in that particular organ years ago.

It was just a kiss, dumbass, giving himself a mental head slap as he turned the corner to start the push up the street to where her house stood at the top of the long, busy road. He just needed to have her, have sex. He'd have her, as he'd promised, in his bed, in his arms—on top, underneath, in any permutation possible—and when he'd got her out of his system, which should take a week, he'd be on his way. He would explain, as he always did, that he was only out for a good time, and that he didn't believe in any of those sticky strings that women liked to wrap around things. Then he'd leave without a backward glance and go to Rio or Patagonia and not give her another thought.

"Are you following me?"

Jed whirled around and there she was, running next to him, her wavy, midnight hair hidden by her plain black ball cap pulled low over her eyes. A ten second scan told him everything he needed to know; a pink and orange crop top, soft shoulders dotted with perspiration, a flat stomach, brief, black gym pants that ended mid-thigh. Those long, spectacular legs… She looked like a poster girl for a fitness ad and Jed watched, unamused, when a small group of male joggers whistled at her from across the road. He wasn't sure what irritated him more, the fact that men stumbled over their feet at her long, lean body or that she'd snuck up on him.

"You need to wear more clothes," he growled, shortening his stride to accommodate hers.

"Seriously, what are you doing here?" McKenna demanded.

"Running?"

"Why here, why in my neighborhood?"

"Is there a law against running in your neighborhood?" He gestured to a couple who were plodding along on the other side of the road. "Do you need special dispensation?"

He saw her shoulders rise and slump. "No, of course not…I was just surprised to see you here, on *my* route, in *my* area."

Okay, she was sounding slightly paranoid. Odd.

He saw the uncertain look she sent him and frowned. She seemed a little off-balance and when she pushed her cap away from her face to run the back of her wrist over her forehead, he saw that her makeup free face looked pale in the morning sunlight and her light green eyes were accessorized by blue stripes. He scanned her again, ignoring the sexy body and this time he noted the tight shoulders, the tapping foot, the clenched fist on her hip. It was also obvious that McKenna had little to no sleep last night. Jed wondered what was keeping her awake at all hours. And whatever it was, it wasn't good.

"What's the problem, Legs?"

McKenna darted a look at him and lifted her hands in that age old expression of confusion. Except that he could read body language at a thousand yards and he noticed the jerk of her head and the way that her muscles tightened in her neck. She was good, for an amateur but he was a damn good professional.

"Why on earth would you think that there's a problem?" she demanded.

"Honey, you can't lie for shit," Jed told her, as they turned the corner to power up the hill that led to her house. "You're wound tighter than a spring, you haven't slept—you probably haven't slept well in weeks—and I'm following you because I happen to be jogging in the same direction as you?"

Her cheeks flushed an even deeper pink. "Maybe I'm just flustered because you kissed me."

Jed snorted his disbelief. He'd encountered skilled liars in every corner of the world, did she really expect him to believe that crock of shit? "Legs, as hot as that kiss was and it was nuclear, you're not the type to go weird over a kiss or, regrettably, a man. Nope, something else has you all hot and bothered."

McKenna didn't answer him and Jed narrowed his eyes. "I can't help you if you don't tell me."

McKenna put on a burst of speed and Jed easily followed her up the last hill, stopping when the ground leveled out, which happened to be outside of her house. With her back to it, she placed her hands on her knees and looked up at him, those fabulous eyes sparking. "*Nothing* is wrong and I don't *need* your help."

Jed looked at the front door and tracked his eyes across the front of the house, abruptly stopping when he looked at the bay window of the salon, the one he'd stood at yesterday. Except today there was a massive hole in the glass pane.

"No problems, huh?" Jed nodded to the broken window and heard her swift intake of breath.

"What the hell…?"

Cursing, Jed hopped over the low wrought iron fence and walked across the stones pavers that ran up to the house. It was second nature to preserve evidence, such as fingerprints and also not to leave any of his own so Jed whipped his T-shirt off, folded it and laid it on the sill. Trying to avoid the glass shards, he boosted himself up, holding his weight on his forearms to peer through the hole in the pane.

He felt the bite of glass in the ball of his hand but he ignored it to make sense of the room. A brick lay in the middle of the room, the obvious source of the broken glass. But why were there reddish-brown streaks on the carpet and handprints in the same color on the wedding dresses hanging on a rack? Jed felt his heartbeat increase and his vision focused. The light was dim but the color looked like blood…and it looked like there was a lot of it. His first thought was of Daisy, that she could be hurt.

JesusGodinHeaven. He dropped back to the ground and whirled around to look at McKenna, who was standing on the pathway, fear and horror on her face.

Jed took two steps and grabbed McKenna's shoulders,

squeezing to get her quick and immediate attention. "Where's Daisy?"

It took her a moment to answer and Jed was on the point of giving her a quick shake when she opened her mouth to speak. "At school...she's at school," McKenna said in a shaky voice. "I drove her there, it's down the road and I started my run from there. I was going to run back to my car and drive home."

"And was anyone else inside?" Jed demanded. Daisy was fine and McKenna was standing in front of him. Also fine. His heart could resume beating. "Mattie?"

"No."

Jed's mind moved at supersonic speed. Okay, there was no need to bash the door down to check for injured people. He kept one hand on her shoulder as he turned to look at the broken window. "I'm presuming that this was intact when you left to take Daisy to school?"

McKenna nodded, her eyes fixed on the mess in front of her.

"So, sometime in the last forty-five minutes, someone broke your window and trashed your salon, pouring something that is supposed to look like blood over your floor, furniture, and painting the wedding dresses hanging on the rack with it."

McKenna let out a low, painful moan and Jed's hand tightened on her shoulder. "So, let me ask you this again...what's the problem?"

Chapter Four

McKenna, now dressed in a pair of skinny jeans, said goodbye to the police officer and watched as he walked out of her salon, Jed two steps behind him. McKenna wrapped her hands around her abdomen and grabbed the edges of her silk T-shirt, desperate to hold onto something, anything. The hang up calls she could handle, the stupid emails she could ignore but someone—Craig?—tossed a brick through her window and broke into her house. Jed found the window to the downstairs bathroom open and footsteps in the flower bed told him, and the police, the window was the intruder's point of entry and his goal was to smear red paint all over her salon.

McKenna couldn't look at the destroyed dresses. Luckily they were just samples, but she often hung wedding dresses on the rack that were ready to be collected. It could've been a bride's precious dress that got destroyed. God, she'd dodged a career destroying bullet.

McKenna shoved her shaking hands under her thighs, hoping the pressure would stop the trembling. Fear raced up and down her spine and she felt bilious. God, what had she done to deserve this? She'd joined Craig on two dates and she'd behaved appropriately; no flirting, no innuendos, no offers, and certainly no promises. She'd done nothing—nothing!—to warrant the phone calls and the email messages, and they were hard enough to deal with, but the fact that someone, a malicious someone, had been in her home, amongst her stuff, the home she shared with her innocent and defenseless daughter, kicked her fear into higher gear. Had he gone into their bedrooms? Had he sat on her bed? Had he touched her lingerie, Daisy's toys?

McKenna's stomach contracted and she swallowed the bile she tasted in the back of her throat.

McKenna resisted the urge to put her head between her legs and forced herself to think. He hadn't had that much time and Jed, and the policeman, told her there was no indication that he went upstairs, that he went into any other room but the salon. *Focus on that. Don't let your imagination go wild. Be sensible and think. You have to find a way to deal with this, hopefully to stop it. But how? What could she do?*

God, she'd never felt more alone in her life.

The door opened and closed behind her and without needing to turn, she knew Jed was back. He shifted energy and his presence made her feel stronger and more in control. That was weird; nobody had ever had the ability to calm her jangled nerves by simply walking into the room.

"I asked Mattie to bring you some coffee," Jed stated, leaning his shoulder into the wall and crossing his arms across his broad chest.

Even in running shorts and the plain black T-shirt he'd taken off earlier—his body had, momentarily distracted her from the break in—he exuded power and control. Some men needed three thousand dollar suits and a fancy title; this photographer just needed to lift one dark eyebrow to get his point across. *I want answers and I want them now.*

Unfortunately, McKenna didn't know where to start…

Jed seemed to read her mind. "At the beginning," he suggested. "Tell me what you told the police."

"They said that they probably won't find any fingerprints," McKenna mused, trying to postpone the conversation. Talking about the situation made it feel more real, and it was plenty real already.

"Probably not. Start talking, McKenna."

McKenna looked at the broken window and wondered if he'd understand if she told him that she'd felt a little lonely, isolated, and bored and that, maybe, she should start meeting men again. Just for some laughs, some company, an orgasm or two. Normal men, successful men, non-crazy making men.

From the outside, Craig had seemed perfect. He was the fiancé of one of her first clients and she'd liked him, thought him attractive. When he and Haley broke their engagement six months later, she accepted his offer for dinner and the first date had been…okay. He seemed to be a nice, normal guy so she agreed to a second date and afterward she'd allowed him to kiss her at the door. By the time she reached her bedroom fifteen minutes later, she'd received three text messages and two declarations of something that sounded close to love. Immediately spooked, she'd ignored the messages, switched her phone off. The next morning she'd endured a three minute lecture on why she should never be unavailable to him.

When she became president of the world she would make a ruling that all men had to have a label attached to the back of their necks. Misogynistic, arrogant, psycho….

Two dates three months back and the phone calls and text messages had been unceasing. The sour cherry on this rotten cake was that Haley and Craig had reconciled. She was once again a client and when Craig accompanied her to the salon, he acted like the perfect, charming fiancé and like butter wouldn't melt in his mouth.

She had to suck up her desire to strip sixteen layers of skin off him because she had no proof that it was Craig; the emails came from a generic account and the phone calls came from different cellular numbers. And, to the town, he was a well-liked and well respected and nobody would believe her.

She was, basically, screwed. And not in a good way.

"Someone tossed a brick through your window and broke into your home, Dixon," Jed said on a low growl, interrupting her panicked thoughts. "Who have you pissed off lately?"

Jed straightened at the knock on the door. He walked across the room to let Mattie, who was carrying a tray, inside. McKenna sent her an anxious glance. "Thanks, Matt."

Mattie smiled and placed the tray on the table by the window. She looked at the ruined dresses and grimaced. "Ugh. And that beading was hand sewn and hell on the fingers."

Jed frowned as he walked across the room to join them.

"You made that gown?"

"I make all the gowns designed by McKenna," Mattie replied. "She designs them, I make them."

Jed took the cup of black coffee that McKenna held out to him and she felt sparks shoot up her arm when their fingers made brief contact. God, she was far too old to be so ridiculous.

"Okay." Jed sipped, frowned and sipped again. "So you two are a partnership?"

"Yes," McKenna replied at the same time that Mattie shook her head. Mattie shook her head at McKenna and she waited for the words that she knew were coming.

"McKenna owns the business; it's her name and cachet that bring people to the door." Mattie sent Jed a bright smile.

Jed's big hand almost swallowed the fragile china cup and his finger tapped against the rim. "Can you think of anyone who might like to mess with McKenna?" he asked Mattie.

"Apart from the guy she went on two dates with and who started hassling her straight afterward?" Mattie dropped into a chair and crossed her legs.

New shoes, McKenna realized, and designer, too. Nice. McKenna stared at Mattie's black-and-cream Mary Jane platforms and waited for Jed's explosion. It didn't come, so she lifted his eyes to his face. A muscle ticked in his jaw and his eyes narrowed but those were the only indications that he was annoyed.

"She didn't mention him," Jed told Mattie in a cold,

hard voice.

"You haven't given me much of a chance," McKenna pointed out.

"Well, we can't prove it's him but we're pretty sure it is. With him being a big deal in town and the fiancé of one of our most influential clients, it gets a bit tricky," Mattie explained.

"Start," Jed said through clenched teeth. "From the beginning."

When she finished her very brief explanation, Jed pushed an exasperated hand through his hair. "And you told the police officer all this?"

McKenna nodded. "For all the good it'll do."

Mattie jumped into the conversation. "The reason she's been reticent to mention it before now is because I checked with a friend of mine who is a police officer. It seems that without solid proof, and there is none, there's little they can do."

Even though Jed's attention was now off her, McKenna couldn't stop looking at him. His intensity fascinated her; he had the ability to see a problem and want to fix it. Self-confident, fearless, and slightly ferocious.

Jed rested his hip against the table and gave Mattie a perfunctory smile. "Would you excuse us?"

Mattie frowned and her lips pursed. "You want me to leave?"

"Yeah."

"But I'm her best friend, her family," Mattie protested.

Jed didn't ask again but just continued to hold her hot

look. Within twenty seconds, Mattie was unfurling her legs and standing and within another ten, she was walking out of the room, her chin in the air. McKenna sighed; her cousin's feathers were so easily ruffled and she knew that she would hear something later about Jed being domineering and bossy and who did he think he was? Jed waited until the door closed behind her and then he turned that hot glare onto her. "You've got problems, Legs."

Sure, and the biggest one is that if I don't do you, soon, I might explode. McKenna closed her eyes in dismay. She had a stalker who'd escalated to breaking and entering and that was where she was going, straight to getting naked in the bedroom?

"You have no idea," she muttered, mostly to herself.

Jed paced the area in front of her mirrors, oblivious to his tri-reflection. McKenna had to look away; one Jed was hard enough to handle, three was sensory overload.

"My gut is screaming."

McKenna frowned at his murmured comment. "Is that a good or a bad thing?" she inquired.

"Both." Jed stopped pacing and glared at the broken window. "It's a good warning system but it's a bad thing because I know that, as sure as shit, something bad is on its way."

McKenna made herself laugh away the fear that danced down her spine. "I'm thinking you're being a tad dramatic, Hamilton, and letting your imagination run away with you." McKenna waved her hand at the broken window. "Yeah, Craig Daniels is a pain in my ass but this—" she pointed to her paint splattered dresses "—this is a reach. I bet if they check they'll find out that he's in court or in his office. This was probably just kids letting off steam."

God, she hoped so. Please let it be so.

"Or a kid that he hired." Jed glared at her. "And I'm never dramatic. My gut instinct saved my ass more times in dicey situations than I can count," he said, his tone as sharp as the shards of glass on the carpet. "Both on the battlefield and off—"

"You served?" McKenna asked, intrigued. Now that didn't surprise her, he looked like he could handle himself. She also just knew, instinctively that he would've joined a special group, he was not a rank and file type of man. "Army? Navy? Were you a Marine or a SEAL?"

Jed let out a derisive snort at her suggestions. "Please."

"Come on, give me a hint."

"Not going there."

His unwillingness to talk about his past was just a confirmation that he'd done some hard time in the military, that he'd seen some bad stuff. He had super-secret, hard as nails written all over him.

"As I was saying," Jed continued, "you have a stalker who is escalating in violence and you are his target." He shook his head and frowned. "That's a crappy situation to be in."

She'd figured that out but she didn't need him confirming the obvious.

"You need protection."

"I'll be fine," McKenna protested. Seeing his disbelieving expression, she lifted one shoulder. "I just need some time to figure out a way to handle this."

"Time you might not have." Jed whirled around and snatched the photograph that was lying face down on the desk. Her stalker had left it there and McKenna had been trying not to think of it. He held it up; she saw the image and gulped. It was of picture of her, lying on a beach, with a knife plunged into her chest.

"You can't be fine if you're dead."

His blunt, factual statement made her haul in a breath. Okay, there was that.

"And it's not just about you, there's a child living in this house, too."

McKenna pushed her fist into her stomach and closed her eyes. Daisy; her life, her treasure, the reason the sun rose every morning. He was right, of course he was. She knew she could take her chances with her own life but she would never, never risk Daisy's. It didn't matter how small the risk was, in relation to Daisy, it was unacceptable. She'd lock them into a *Doomsday Preppers* basement for months if that was what it took to keep her safe.

Squaring her shoulders, she looked at Jed. "Okay, point taken. Maybe I should find someone who can protect us until we get some answers."

Jed's face remained impassive but she sensed, rather than saw, him sucking in his breath. "Or I can do it."

"Uh..." Whoo boy. The man just had to be in the same room and he made her feel jangly and weird, she didn't know if she could live in the same house as him.

She latched onto the first excuse she could find. "I think

I need someone who specializes in bodyguarding."

Jed's glance raked her from tip to toe and his golden eyes warmed. "I *can* do it."

She knew that he could do *that,* and with some skill, too, but keeping her and Daisy safe from danger, maybe not so much. The guy was a *photographer,* she reminded herself. "I'm sure that you think you can but you have been a photographer for a long time—ten years is it?—and I'm sure your soldier skills are rusty."

The corners of Jed's mouth lifted and the hint of a dimple appeared in his cheek. "Have you been checking up on me, Mac?"

Her dad used to call her Mac, McKenna remembered. Nobody did anymore and she'd forgotten how much she liked it. And yes, she had Googled him. He'd had seven assignments for the magazine, had made the cover twice and was known to be one of the most exciting and adventurous photographers in the world right now. While his name wasn't quite a household one, like some of the older photographers working for the same magazine were, McKenna was convinced that it wouldn't be long until he joined their ranks.

"The British government spent millions training me; it's not something that I will ever forget."

McKenna tipped her head, confused. "You're not American?"

"Dual citizenship; my mother was from the UK. I joined the British Army, partly to piss my father off, partly because I wanted to join their spec ops community," Jed calmly stated. "I haven't committed to my next assignment, I'm in place and I will keep both of you safe. And I'll help you get to the bottom of this."

"I can't ask you to do that," McKenna protested. But, dear God, she wanted to. Despite the crazy attraction arcing between them she knew, in that deep female part of her, in her soul, that he would do exactly what he said. She and Daisy would be safe with him.

"You're not asking, I'm offering," Jed pointed out. "I need to go back to my place to collect some clothes and my laptop. When we get back I'll help you clean this place up."

McKenna looked around at her once beautiful, now ruined salon. "I'll have to re-carpet and repaint the walls. Recover the furniture. Dammit, they managed to get paint on everything!"

"I think that was the point," Jed said, his tone dry.

"Why don't you just go and I'll start work here?" McKenna gestured to the books on the floor, the bridal magazines that had been ripped apart and whose pages were scattered across the carpet, some stuck together with paint.

"The point of having a bodyguard is to guard your body. I can't do that if we're apart so where you go, I go and vice versa." Jed jerked his head to the door and McKenna reluctantly stood up. "How safe is Daisy's school? What is the access like?"

McKenna walked into the hall and reached for her bag that was hanging on a hook. "Tight. Only Mattie and I can collect her or drop her off and you can't just wander in."

Jed nodded and pulled open the front door, guiding her

through with a hand on her back. They stood on the front step and McKenna noticed a big, black, kickass SUV parked in front of the house. "That yours?" she asked.

"Yep. I asked Leah to deliver it for me while we were busy with the police," Jed explained, opening the front passenger door for her. She climbed up into the seat and he slammed the door closed behind her. McKenna watched him in the side mirror, before he crossed the street he looked around, his glance seemingly casual but she knew his concentration was absolute. He looked like a predator, a hunter, alert and very, very dangerous.

She liked the fact that he was on her side; the same feminine intuition that insisted that she and Daisy were safe with him was also telling her he would be lethal to have as an enemy.

★ ★ ★

MCKENNA WALKED AHEAD of Jed into his one-bedroom apartment and looked around. That took about three seconds. There was a long, comfortable couch, a mammoth, flat screen TV, and a massive pile of books against one wall. He'd been meaning to build a bookshelf for years but had never got around to it. He'd also considered hiring a decorator to make it look more like a home, to put some art up on the walls, to choose some decent furniture, but that had failed to happen, too. Besides, what was the point of shelling out a pot of cash for stuff that would never be used? Unlike his other properties which were income generating, this apartment was just a dust catcher.

McKenna placed her bag on the counter that separated the lounge from the small kitchen and hopped up onto a barstool. She dragged a finger across the counter top and Jed was glad he'd run a rag over it before he left for his run. His apartment might look like a monk's cell, but at least she couldn't accuse him of being a dirty slob. Jed did a mental head shake. It was stupid to be concerned about what this woman thought about him or his apartment; it had been a long times since he cared about someone's opinion and couldn't understand why now and why her.

And, crap, what was he thinking, offering his time to protect her? The reasonable, sensible part of him thought he was insane—it didn't look like she was hurting for money and could pay for protection and he should be concentrating on sorting Leah out so that he could head down to Venezuela. But he wasn't going to do that, he'd shot his mouth off and told her that he'd keep her safe.

Bat.

Shit.

Insane.

"I'm going to have a quick shower and shove some clothes in a bag," he told her, resisting the urge to run this hand over the knobs that he could see of her spine, through her thin, pale pink silk T-shirt. He nodded to his state of the art coffee machine. "Help yourself."

"Thanks." McKenna rested her head in the palm of her hand, looking smaller and suddenly exhausted.

Jed found himself leaning forward to pull her against

him, to wrap his arms around her, and to reassure her that she would be fine. He wanted to chase those shadows out of her eyes, put some color back into her cheeks.

Then he remembered how her mouth tasted and he started imagining her wet and soapy in the shower with him, her head tipped back against the tiles as he sucked water from her nipples, from between her legs. Pulling himself from the fantasy, he hauled in a deep breath thinking this entire situation was out of control. And, instead of running as far and as fast as he could from it, every time he opened his big mouth he complicated his life further.

Oh, fuck it, he was losing his mind. It was the only explanation he could come up with. Striding across the room, he walked into his bedroom and slammed the door behind him. Pulling off his shirt as he walked into the bathroom, he tossed it toward the laundry basket and hopped up onto the edge of the tub. Grabbing the top of the bathroom door, he pulled it toward him and dipped his hand into the large cavity he'd cut out in the edge of the door. It was fifteen inches long, nearly as wide as the door and ten inches deep. He pulled out an H&K and two magazines. Tucking the spare magazine under his arm, he slammed the other into the pistol and quickly sent a round into the chamber. He flicked the safety on and placed it within easy reach on the counter next to the basin. He instantly felt better and a lot more in control. Leaving the wad of cash, a credit card, a burner phone, and a fake identity in place, he stepped down from the tub and looked up at the door and thought it was a bloody good hiding place, better than the safe in the bedroom. He had other hiding places around the apartment and around the world.

He believed in being prepared, he thought, as he opened the door to the bathroom cabinet. He picked up an unopened box of condoms and checked the expiry date.

In every way that mattered.

Chapter Five

JED WAS SHOVING a pile of T-shirts into a bag on his bed and he turned at the sound of her footsteps. Seeing his querying expression she lifted her hands. "I need to use your bathroom, is that okay?"

"Sure." Jed lifted his chin toward the bathroom and McKenna walked into his room, sliding past him toward the en suite bathroom.

After doing the necessary, McKenna washed her hands and noticed the droplets of water on the mirror and the image of him, wet and naked, popped onto the big screen of her mind. Ah, God. This was killing her. Splashing herself with cold water, she reached for the hand towel next to the basin and buried her face into the slightly damp folds. She could smell him on the towel as well, and she let out a low groan.

"You okay?" Jed called. Trust the man to have ears like a bat.

"Fine," McKenna replied, dropping the towel. Shoving her hands into the back pockets of her jeans, she walked back into his bedroom and looked around. "You're not a nester, are you?"

Jed looked like she'd accused him of wearing girly panties. "A what?"

"A nester…someone who likes making a home, who collects stuff."

Jed looked around. "Uh…that would be a no. I'm never in one place for more than a couple of weeks so I've never really bothered. I'm not big on…stuff."

McKenna leaned her shoulder into the doorframe. "I can see that," she said, her tone dry.

"I presume that you are a nester." Jed walked into the closet and his voice became slightly muffled.

"I have a child, it's part of the deal." McKenna shrugged. "Do you have any kids?"

"God, no," Jed snapped back. When he came back out, he held some socks in his hand and a pair of expensive sneakers dangled from his fingertips. "My lifestyle is not conducive to a family, kids, a relationship. I am a here today, gone tomorrow kind of guy."

Okay, that was easily interpreted. *Don't even consider looking at me for anything long-term.* His warning wasn't necessary; she'd worked that out for herself already.

McKenna couldn't meet his eyes, so she looked around, and on his bed was the distinctive aqua border of the iconic magazine. Stepping toward the bed, she reached across and snagged the magazine, knowing it had to be a new edition as it had a black and white cover that she didn't recognize.

McKenna looked down at the photograph and her lungs stopped functioning. Jed's eyes dominated the image, yellow gold and filled with fury. His mouth was a slash in his face and from his crouched position he looked like a sleek panther, all power and rage waiting for a place to explode. McKenna shifted her focus off Jed's streaked with dust, but still compelling, face and took in the rest of the details; two small heads were burrowed into Jed's chest, his broad hands resting on slight, young, far-too-skinny backs covered with paper thin shirts.

Jed was holding two children and he was about to unleash a world of hurt onto whoever was threatening them. The image was intensely powerful and incredibly evocative; she could taste the dust in her throat, the heat shimmering off the dirt road, could feel the tension of the crowd gathered behind Jed. She wanted to flip the pages to read the story, to find out what happened next....and that, she realized, was the point of a great cover.

"Holy crackers," she said before finally looking at him.

Jed looked thoroughly pissed off. "I've had a couple of photos make the cover but I never wanted to be in any of the damn things," he stated, his voice a low rumble and threaded with frustration. "h I begged but they refused to change the cover."

"They were right not to, it's a powerful image." McKenna sat on the edge of the bed and placed the magazine in her lap. "Where were you?" she asked, tracing the sides of the publication with her index finger.

"India," Jed replied, his tone terse.

McKenna heard his loud sigh and when she looked at him, he crossed his arms and sent her a defiant look, as if daring her to ask for more information. She'd never backed down from a dare in her life. "You're just going to leave me hanging?"

Jed nodded to the magazine. "The story, for what's it worth, is in there."

"I'd rather hear it from you. Come on," she cajoled, handing him an encouraging smile, "it won't hurt."

"Shit," Jed muttered, raking his hand through is hair. "Okay…"

McKenna knew if she spoke again, she'd lose him, so she just waited for him to continue, somehow knowing Jed rarely explained anything to anybody. She couldn't help feeling a little warm and slightly fuzzy at the notion of this taciturn and slow talking man opening up to her. Slow talking, McKenna mused, taking the thought and turning it over. Talking slow was just another indication of his confidence, it made people—her—hang off his every word.

"Short story; India, two kids, being beaten in the street by someone who I presume was their grandmother. When I say beaten, I mean beaten with a solid branch maybe three inches wide. The magazine had sent an intern—" There was an infinitesimal pause before he said the word "intern" and the corners of his eyes tightened and she knew, she just knew, he'd just lied to her. "—and I saw this and I couldn't stand by and watch. I handed my camera to the intern and I ripped the club from her hand. The kids launched themselves at me and my intern took the photograph. It was never meant to be sent to New York with the rest of my photos."

She was pretty sure that Jed never meant to do anything that he shouldn't. "You didn't check them before you sent them off?"

"It's not unusual for photojournalists to shoot many thousands of photos per assignment. I must have missed it," Jed smoothly replied. This time the pinch of his eyes was even quicker and if she hadn't been looking so carefully for it, she would've missed it. Damn, but the guy lied well.

She sent him a disbelieving look. "Crap," she told him.

Those dark eyebrows lifted and his hands, busy zipping his bag, stilled. "Sorry?"

"I think your nose just grew about an inch," McKenna told him, linking her hands around her knee. "But you are a very good liar."

"You think I'm *lying*?"

She had to grin at the affront in his voice. McKenna was pretty certain no one ever challenged him and this was a new experience. *Good, new experiences were excellent for personal growth.* "I know that you are lying." McKenna grinned as his eyes narrowed. "Oh, I think the story about the kids is true, but the story about the intern is bogus and you're not the type to forget a damn thing so that doesn't ring true."

Jed just stared at her and he looked so uncomfortable that McKenna reached across the bed to pat his hand. "You okay, there, bud?"

Jed sent her a hot, annoyed glance and snatched his hand away. "Why wouldn't I be?"

McKenna straightened and then climbed to her feet. She tipped her head and sent him a pitying look. "I just thought you might be feeling disconcerted because I called you on telling me porkies."

"I wasn't lying and I sure as hell am not disconcerted,"

Jed muttered, ducking around the side of the bed to approach her.

There was that hot, predatory look again and her spine readied itself for her nerves to explode into tiny bundles of fireworks. She could smell soap, fresh and citrusy, toothpaste, and a scent that was all him. Unknowingly she licked her lips and stared at that mobile mouth, longing to reach up and touch his golden stubble.

She forced her brain to work. Jed needed to know that she wasn't just another dumb floozy who would lie down at his command and let him scratch her tummy. "Of course you are; you're used to being believed, being the focus of attention, to having your ego stroked...especially by women."

Jed's head jerked back and McKenna knew she'd struck a chord. If she couldn't have him, and she couldn't, then she wanted, at the very least, his truths, or nothing at all.

"I have no idea what you're prattling on about," Jed growled. "Maybe I should make you shut up."

"Distract and duck the subject." McKenna made herself say the words, even though her tongue had thickened and her pulse was pounding. All because he'd put his hands on her hips and was staring at her mouth. She tipped her head back and stared up and into those compelling, wild eyes. "You're not that hard to read, Hamilton."

Jed's fingers tightened on her hips. "You think you can read me, Legs?"

If I can get my brain to work, McKenna silently replied. Instead of voicing those thoughts, which would inflate that already monstrous ego, she pushed back and placed some space between them. Jed would only allow her to retreat five inches but that was better than having her breasts pushing into his hard chest, his hard erection against her stomach. She could get a little oxygen to her brain…

"You're a guy, you're not that difficult," McKenna scoffed.

"Go for it," Jed stated, his tone unconcerned but she noted the wariness in his eyes.

McKenna stepped away and Jed dropped his hands, shoving them into the front pockets of his jeans. "You're rough and tough and you never qualify yourself because the only opinion that matters is your own. I'm surprised that you bothered to lie to me, normally you wouldn't because you don't give a toss what people think. You are a rule breaker and competitive, calculating and focused. You also have a protective instinct a mile wide, judging by your immediate defense of those kids and your jumping in to help a woman you don't know from a danger we're not sure is real or not."

"It's real."

McKenna ignored his interruption. "Am I right?"

"Leah wants you to make her wedding dress so I have to make sure that nothing happens to you."

Nice try, Hamilton. "You don't even want Leah to get married, Jed, so that excuse won't wash. I figure it's one of two things; you're either naturally protective or you want to keep me safe so that you can get into my pants."

"I just want to get into your pants," Jed shot back.

Me thinks the hottie doth protest too much...

Jed's next words blew her smug attitude away. "The pants feeling is mutual."

McKenna blushed and wished she could deny his accusation. She also wished she could be certain that she could resist him. She wasn't. She sighed her frustration. "Yeah, unfortunately I do."

Jed took a step toward her and she immediately raised her hand in a "down, boy" gesture. "Except that it's not going to happen, Slick."

"You've really got to stop lying to yourself." Jed lifted one arrogant eyebrow.

McKenna narrowed her eyes before sighing. "Ok...I'm not sure that it isn't going to happen. Happy now?"

"No, I'd be happier if you were naked and panting my name."

McKenna ignored his statement and the resultant images that seared her brain. Instead, she tipped her head up to look at the ceiling. "If, and that's a big if, I decide to sleep with you, then you should know that I'm not going to expect anything from you except some really good sex."

How the hell had they gone from her challenging him about lying to having a discussion about the sex that they might or might not—but probably would—have?

She dropped her head to look at him and he blinked, this time openly surprised. "Say what?"

Oh well, she couldn't feel any more embarrassed, so she'd might as well just get the rest of it out.

"Sex. I expect it to be good and for you to be discreet, I

have a child in the house and I do not want her to find you in my bed in the mornings. I do not do anything weird…"

Jed looked amused. "Define weird."

She was burning up from the inside out. "I'll let you know if you cross the line."

Jed inched his way closer. "You do that."

"Oh, and it would be, a two, maybe three-week deal," McKenna gabbled, placing her hand on his chest to keep him from kissing her. If he kissed her, she'd be lost.

"What's a three-week deal?" Jed asked, lifting his hand to hold the side of her face. She groaned a deep, sexy sound in the back of her throat when he brushed his thumb across her lower lip.

"You and me, living with me, this protecting my body nonsense," McKenna stated, her eyes on his mouth. She was done with talking; she wanted him kissing her…now. Immediately.

On her face, Jed's hand tightened. "I'm not putting a time limit on your safety," he told her, his tone steel hard.

"And I'm not prepared for this to go on forever," McKenna retorted.

She knew, instinctively, that she couldn't afford to live with Jed, sleep with Jed, for an extended period. Her heart, that foolish stupid organ, had no sense of self-preservation and she could run the risk of feeling more for him than she should. She was already far too attracted to him for her own sanity and she knew that having him around long-term was dangerous.

Not only for her, but for Daisy, too. Yes, Daisy went to a

play group but she still spent a lot of time at home and, with Jed living with them, she'd have far too much contact with him. McKenna didn't want Daisy getting attached to Jed, to seeing him as the daddy she so desperately wanted. Hell, McKenna didn't want to get attached either. Two heart wrenching, tear creating love affairs with men who couldn't love her the way she needed to be loved were enough for one person in one lifetime…she wouldn't risk her heart again.

Not that there was an icicle's chance in a sauna that Jed would fall in love with her—God, he was so not the type—but she couldn't take the chance.

So it would be better to corral her restless libido, start thinking like a responsible adult, and walk away. Now, right now.

It would be the sensible, adult, clever decision.

"Maybe we should rethink this, just slow this down a bit," McKenna quickly said. "I think we're moving a bit too fast."

Jed gave her a hard stare. She expected him to argue, to call her a tease, but he just gave one sharp nod before speaking again. "With or without sex, I'm staying for as long as you and Daisy aren't safe."

"That won't work for me," McKenna told him, feeling panicky. He was too big, too overwhelming to live with on an ongoing basis.

Jed shrugged and reached for his bag, casually slinging it over his shoulder. "Deal with it." He bent his knees so that his face was level with hers. "Oh, and Legs?"

"What?"

"We will be sleeping together. Sooner rather than later."

McKenna's jaw locked at the confidence in that statement. She knew it was pride that made her chin lift, her eyes narrow, and her voice cool. "When hell freezes over."

"Keep telling yourself that, darling, if it makes you feel better." Jed grabbed her hand and pulled her toward the door of the bedroom. "Just an FYI, if we stay in here for ten more seconds, it'll be a lot sooner."

At the doorway, McKenna looked over her shoulder at the big bed and wished that she was in it. Naked with Jed looming over her, sliding into her.

Ack.

She was in such trouble.

LIKE EVERYTHING ELSE he'd been trained to do over the past fifteen years, falling asleep was something Jed did easily. It didn't matter where he was, whether it was on an airplane or in a cave, standing up or sitting, if he decided he needed to sleep then he'd sleep. He didn't lie awake staring at the ceiling; he'd trained himself to have complete mastery over his mind and his body.

Until last night, Jed thought, staring into the cup of black coffee on the kitchen table in front of him. Last night his training had deserted him because he'd stared up at that ceiling for hours, his thoughts in turmoil and his body begging him to walk down the hall and find McKenna. He hadn't, but he'd come damn close, once, twice, fifteen times.

He still had control over his little brain, thank God. Over anything else to do with Legs, he wasn't so sure. Unfortunately, he knew what he was so freaked out about...

Yesterday, during their conversation in his bedroom, she'd looked at him and he realized that it had been a long time since anybody had called him on his bullshit. She'd picked up on the fact that he was lying about that intern—it had been another Pytheon operative, Bryn—and he hadn't forgotten to delete that photo. He'd been crisscrossing the Indian subcontinent looking for the suspected leader of a human trafficking ring, specializing in children, and he suspected that his defense of those kids put him on someone's radar. After the incident, he was constantly followed and his gut instinct told him to dump the evidence of his surveillance. He didn't take the time to sort through his photos, some were for the magazine, some were of his target and his henchmen. He'd just uploaded them all to the Pytheon server for the analysts to sort out, wiping the camera's memory. At his request, the Pytheon geeks sent the relevant photos onto the magazine, including, and stupidly, the photo Bryn had snapped.

The point was that McKenna knew, instinctively, that he'd lied and that worried him. He'd erected walls around his true self for a reason; he was more effective in both his careers if he kept people at a distance, if he remained emotionally removed. Another part of him, the part that wanted to keep him standing on the earth and breathing, didn't like the fact that he'd given himself away and to a civilian to boot. And he hated the fact that every time he came close to her, it felt like she was shoving her hand into his chest cavity, rooting around to attack his heart.

He'd wanted to tell her the long version of that story, explain how furious he'd been at the abuse and how much he wanted to pull those kids—so thin, so scared—out of that situation, how helpless he'd felt when they'd belted out of his arms after a sharp order from a man on the side-lines and run into the crowd. They'd melted away as they'd been taught to do. Child thieves, caught up in a situation they couldn't control.

Possible, probable, *easy*, targets for the man he was watching.

He'd felt useless and impotent and so damn angry. He'd shrugged it off, returned to work, but as soon as he'd been alone he placed his fist into the thin wall of his scummy hotel room. The desire to tell McKenna had been strong but he'd swallowed it down, knowing what her reaction would be. Men like him, big, bold, supposedly fearless, weren't supposed to be emotional, vulnerable. Women didn't want that from him. Women expected stoic self-assuredness and he'd played this game before; he'd been accused of being cold and unemotional and then, the one time when he had dared to show a softer side, punished for being vulnerable.

No, talking to McKenna—to any woman about anything that had more depth than a paddling pool—was out of the question. Like everything else, when he learned a lesson he learned it really well.

Jed swiped his finger across the screen of his phone and logged into a highly encrypted program. As one of Pytheon's longest serving and most trusted agents, he had highest security clearance than most and could track the progress of their high priority missions, of which finding Bo Barker was among the top three. Cracker, their white hat hacker had yet to make any progress tracking down the source of the emails, including the one with the video attached, received at Pytheon HQ. Why send it? Why draw attention to yourself? Jed couldn't figure that out. The Recruiter's job was done, Bo Barker was, for now, out of their reach so why brag? Why run that risk? Jed felt that tingle lifting the hairs on the back of his head. They were missing something; he knew it like he knew his own handwriting.

Or maybe, like Seth suggested, he was just over worked and tired, a little burned out. That may be but when he was done in Cape Town, after this situation with McKenna was resolved, he'd return to Pakistan and turn that country upside down until he found Barker and his not-so-merry band of fuckers. When they were discharged—in whatever form that took—he'd take a solid six-month break and take happy shots, photographs that didn't make his heart bleed.

Puppies and rainbows and shit like that. "I hearded the owl."

Jed instinctively pushed his chair backward and was halfway off it when he realized that he'd been spooked by a three-year-old. "Gawd-dammit!"

What was it with these Dixon women's ability to sneak up on him? He was ex-Special Forces for crap's sake, nothing and nobody sneaked, snuck...dammit... surprised him!

"That's another swear word. When my mommy swears

she puts money in a jar."

Hell, if he had to do that, he'd be broke in a week. Soldiers weren't known for their clean mouths and generally believed a word was not a word without being prefixed by the F-bomb. Jed leaned back in his chair and stretched out his legs, looking at Daisy out of the corner of his eye. She looked like everything he'd fought for—freedom, innocence, safety—should look like. Bright, blue eyes and deep, black curls, a little girl dressed in jeans and a simple tee.

"I tolded you…I hearded the owl just now," Daisy insisted and Jed was charmed by her need to add an "ed" onto her verbs.

He leaned forward and shook his head. "I don't think so, Daisy. Owls are nocturnal."

Daisy sent him the strangest look but before she could say anything, McKenna walked into the room and the fabric of his cargo shorts tightened across his groin. He silently groaned. He needed to get laid, and soon.

"Morning." She bent and dropped a kiss into Daisy's hair. "Hey, baby girl. What's cookin', good lookin'?"

Daisy sent her a gap-toothed grin and leaned her head into McKenna's slim thigh, her gaze returning to his face. Jed wanted to squirm at her direct look; he'd faced down terrorists and drug lords with equanimity but this little girl made him nervous.

The big girl did, too.

"It's okay." Daisy reached across the table and patted his hand.

He flicked a look a McKenna who shrugged her confusion. "Uh...what's okay?"

"It's okay if you mix things up. It's not nice to make fun of people," Daisy informed him, her bright eyes filled with sympathy.

Well, that was good to know except he didn't have the first clue what she was talking about.

"I think you're going to have to explain what you mean, honey," McKenna suggested, turning away to the counter to pour herself a cup of coffee.

Daisy sighed and her shoulders slumped. "I told Jed that I heard-ed an owl."

"Heard," McKenna corrected.

"Heard an owl," Daisy repeated the words. "Jed said that I didn't, that it's not a turtle. I know it's not a turtle and I did-heard-ed it!"

Don't let me laugh, Jed begged someone, anyone. *Please don't let me laugh at this gorgeous little girl who would probably never forgive me in a hundred years if I did.* He swallowed, noticed the tremors in McKenna's back and shoulders and swallowed again. He was an excellent, proficient actor but this time it took all his effort to keep his face impassive. He reached across the table and tapped Daisy's hand with one finger until she finally, finally looked at him.

"I didn't say 'not a turtle' I said 'nocturnal.' That means that it only comes out at night and that I didn't think you'd hear it at—" he looked at his watch. "—oh seven hundred in the morning."

Daisy's nose wrinkled in confusion. "Oh seven whattie?"

"Seven o'clock, Daisy," McKenna said. She was now facing him again, cradling a cup of coffee in her hands. Her eyes were still laughing and his warmed looking at her.

Daisy grabbed his finger and squeezed. "So owls are noc…what did you say?"

"Nocturnal." Jed left his finger in her tiny grip. "What type of owl did you think you heard?"

Daisy looked at him like he was a brain cell from being demented. "An owl owl."

"There are different types of owls and they all look different. It could've been a barn owl or an eagle owl."

Daisy whirled around in her seat. "Mommy, I wanna see a barn owl or …or…the other one. Can you show me pictures? Now? On the 'puter?"

Over Daisy's head McKenna sent him a "thanks for nothing" look. "When you get home from swimming, we'll jump on my laptop and see if we find any pictures of the owl."

"And if you hear it again, call me and I'll see if we can see it for real." Jed heard the words coming out of his mouth and wondered if he'd lost his mind. He didn't engage with kids, ever.

Daisy pushed out her bottom lip and her eyes turned stormy. "I don't want to go to swimming."

He heard a soft tap and tipped his head to look under the table. Yep, she was stamping her foot.

"You're going to swimming, Daisy." McKenna's tone didn't change.

Daisy's thunder cloud filled face suggested she was going to throw herself on the floor, but one look from McKenna had her reconsidering that option. Huh. That was one powerful glare. Daisy slapped her arms against her chest and sent him a "pity me" look.

"You don't know how I suffer," she told him before she walked away, carrying the weight of the world on her shoulders.

"Breakfast in ten minutes, Daisy May!" McKenna told her departing back.

Daisy replied by flinging her mother a dirty look over her hunched shoulder.

Jed placed his hand on his heart and looked at McKenna. "I think I'm in love," he told her, on a small grin.

McKenna rolled her eyes. "My daughter has the ability to wrap anyone around her baby finger." McKenna gestured to the fridge. "What do you want for breakfast? There's cereal, yogurt, some fresh strawberries." McKenna opened the fridge to see what else she could offer him.

That didn't even sound like a snack. He was constantly in motion and a high calorie intake kept him fueled so six eggs, bacon, coffee, cheese, toast, and juice was how he always started his day. He'd already done a gym session, cooked and eaten his breakfast, and washed his dishes before he heard the rest of the house stirring.

"I've placed an order for food; it should be delivered later this morning."

"I can feed you," McKenna protested.

Jed's expression turned determined. "You're not paying for my food, Legs." Through the doorway to the hall he could see Daisy sitting on the bottom stairs, arms folded, and looking morose.

"Daisy is not happy," he commented, changing the subject.

McKenna shrugged. "It's Wednesday, we do this dance every Wednesday. Swimming lessons; she hates them. With a passion."

Jed could remember what it felt like having to do something that he loathed. His earliest memories were of being in a car, of being delivered to some practice or another. He'd run from activity to activity and playing with his friends was a foreign concept. His father's approval was dependent on how much he achieved and falling short of the standard, which had always been pretty damn high, was never acceptable. He mentally shuddered at all that wasted effort.

"Don't push her, McKenna," he said, surprised that he'd even go there.

The way McKenna was raising Daisy had nothing to do with him and he didn't have any right to say anything but…God. Even though over thirty years had passed, he still could relate to how Daisy felt.

McKenna took a bowl from the cupboard behind her and pulled out a box of organic muesli from the tall food cupboard in the corner. After dumping some in a bowl, she reached for a banana, peeled it, sliced it and placed it in the bowl. Opening the fridge again, she pulled out some yogurt, organic again, added it to cereal and poured a liberal dose of honey on top.

"Daisy's breakfast," she explained.

"Looks horrible."

"Well, normally I make her scrambled eggs and bacon but someone must have finished what was in the fridge," McKenna replied her voice tart.

Jed grimaced. "Sorry, my bad."

"That amount of cholesterol can't be good for you."

"I burn it off." Jed shrugged away her concern. Okay, so she was ignoring his earlier comment and Jed felt relieved. After all, how she raised her daughter had nothing to do with him.

McKenna called Daisy to eat and returned to the fridge, pulling out a small tub of yogurt before reaching for a spoon. Was that all she was going to eat? That wasn't enough to fuel a fly.

"I'm intrigued that you thought it was necessary to tell me how to raise my child. You are self-contained, almost remote, and you don't strike me as someone who routinely offers an unsolicited opinion. So for you to comment, you obviously feel strongly about the subject," McKenna said, her tone quiet. "Tell me why."

Damn, so he wasn't off the hook. He'd made a habit of keeping his mouth shut, so what the hell had he been thinking? He lifted his hands. "It has nothing to do with me, I shouldn't have said anything."

"Yeah, but you did. And that's why I'm intrigued." McKenna placed a spoon of yogurt in her mouth, turned the spoon over, and slowly pulled it from her mouth. The action was deeply erotic…

"Can we pretend that I didn't say anything and move on?" Jed asked in a strangled tone, his gaze dropping from her mouth to her chest. Today she was wearing a sleeveless black-and-white striped top with a lime-green skirt and high, do-me heels.

"No," McKenna said simply. "You said it, now explain why you would think that I am, from one conversation about swimming, pushing my daughter."

She wasn't going to let him off the hook. "I don't know anything about raising kids, I freely admit that, but I do know what it's like being pushed into doing something that you don't want to do. I can't remember a time that I wasn't doing something, whether it was sports or karate or archery." He lifted one broad shoulder, wishing he could slide into a hole. This very much felt like a personal conversation and he didn't do personal. Or conversations. He'd add one more comment and hopefully that would be the end of it. "I never got to play, like a kid should."

Another lick of her spoon, another contraction in his groin. Watching her eat was so much more fun than talking, and taking her to bed would be the best fun of all.

"Why not?"

Jed gave her a squinty eye. Seriously, they were still on the subject? Jed just took a sip of his cold coffee and ignored her question. He'd said more than enough…

"Conversation over?" McKenna asked and he nodded.

She pursed her lips and he knew she was considering whether to push him. She must've seen the stubborn look on his face because she sighed and scraped the tub with her spoon. She stared at her tub before lifting her eyes to look at him again.

"Swimming is one extramural activity I insist on; mostly because I believe that swimming is a life skill. A few of her play friends have pools and some of the mothers aren't as vigilant as I'd like. If Daze falls in when someone isn't looking, she can save herself."

Okay, that made a whole bunch of sense.

"Unfortunately," McKenna continued, "she's terrified of water and I don't know why. Her instructor is a bit impatient so getting her to swimming is a pain in the ass." McKenna sent him a small smile. "If you plan on coming with us, be prepared for a lot of screeching."

Jed sent her a steady look. "I plan on coming with you; that's what bodyguarding entails."

"Don't say I didn't warn you. It won't be pretty."

Jed watched her walk across the kitchen and out into the hallway, dropping to her haunches to look Daisy in the eye. Her hand reached out to brush a curl off Daisy's cheek and Jed wondered what it would feel like to live normally. A house, a wife, a kid.

It wasn't for him, he'd decided that years ago but, looking at the two dark heads and the love on both faces, he was allowed to wonder. It was, simply, an intellectual exercise. Relationships and commitment equaled, in his head, a loss of freedom and handing over control. Not his thing.

But, damn, he sighed, watching McKenna and Daisy, the picture was damn seductive.

Chapter Six

McKenna sucked in a breath and tried to persuade herself that Leah wasn't dancing on her last nerve. She was the last bride of the day and McKenna was ready to strangle her. Leah had no idea what she wanted in a wedding dress but knew, to the last detail, what she didn't want. Which seemed to be everything McKenna suggested.

Frankly, she'd rather be dragging Daisy, kicking and screaming, to her swimming lessons at this point. Which, she took a quick look at her watch, would be soon. Time to wrap up Miss Picky's appointment and, frankly, it wasn't a moment too soon.

"God, you're a pain in the ass, Lee," Jed said from the doorway. McKenna kept her head down, staring at the picture of the backless dress on her lap, waiting to regain her breath, for her heart rate to subside. Properly ridiculous. She wasn't a silly teenager anymore in the throes of her first crush and she was embarrassed that his voice—his *voice*!—had the ability to make her skin prickle. God, she was so pathetic.

"This is a once-in-a-lifetime dress, Jed, and I'm not going to make a hasty decision," Leah responded and McKenna frowned when she heard the wobble in her voice.

She lifted her head to look at Leah and caught the slight

tremble of Leah's lower lip. Oh, God, there was something brewing here.

"And it would help if my man of honor would give me some help choosing!"

"A—you're not getting married and b—I don't know anything about wedding dresses!" Jed responded, lifting his big hands in frustration. "And one day, a long time in the future, I'll take the photos! At least I won't mess that up."

"You're such a jerk." Leah leapt to her feet and walked over to the bay window and stood with her back to them.

It was ramrod straight but McKenna noticed her trembling knees, the way her fingers clutched and released the fabric at her hips. This wasn't normal bridal nerves, Leah was dealing with something bigger than nerviness.

McKenna stood up, placed the bridal magazine on a side table and slowly, as if she were approaching a skittish horse, walked over to Leah. As she placed her hand in the center of Leah's back, Leah half turned and looked at Jed.

"We're having a small engagement party and I'd like you to be there, Jed. We're having dinner at Diana's, eight o'clock."

Despair chased horror across his face and Leah saw it as clearly as she did. Color leached from her face and her shoulders lifted toward her ears. McKenna saw the tears in her eyes and she expected noisy sobs. However, Leah was made of sterner stuff and McKenna watched as she picked up her composure and locked eyes with her bigger, brawnier, tougher brother.

"Can you please, for one second, get over yourself and

think about me?" she demanded, her voice shaky with emotion. "How dare you, Jed? How dare you waltz back into my life and think that you can just start barking commands, expecting me to jump? You don't know the first thing about me anymore…you don't know me anymore!" Leah sucked in a breath and McKenna shot Jed a quick look. He looked as impassive as ever but she could see the emotion in those eyes, the regret and the confusion.

"You don't know that I'm scared, that I look at Dad and Cruella and wonder if I'm not making the biggest mistake of my life! You don't know how much I miss Mum and how much I wish she was here…I thought—" Leah's voice broke and McKenna swallowed the rapidly increasing lump in her throat. "—I thought that if you did this for me, with me, that I would have a little bit of her with me but all you've done is bitch!" Leah stomped over to the couch and grabbed her bag. "And, frankly, you do that very damn well!"

One solitary tear rolled down Leah's face as she brushed past Jed in the doorway, ignoring his outstretched hand. McKenna closed her eyes as her heavy front door opened and slammed closed. A minute later she heard the deep throttle of Leah's sports car starting. When she looked at Jed she was shocked to see that his face was almost as bloodless as Leah's had been and that he was still staring at her front door as if he were shell-shocked.

It was strange to think that Jed, so utterly masculine and tough and hard-assed, could be felled by a teary eyed blonde.

"Well…" he said, running his hand over the back of his neck and staring at the floor, "…shit." He lifted his head as

McKenna started to speak. "And no, I don't want to talk about it."

Like that was a surprise.

DAISY STARTED CRYING in the car and when she saw the pool, her sobs turned to screams. She was well on her way to being hysterical, McKenna thought, holding the writhing child in her arms. She couldn't make her swim today because Daisy wasn't acting, she wasn't playing up; her child was bone-deep terrified.

Why? McKenna wondered, a headache pounding the back of her skull. Okay, the instructor wasn't warm or fuzzy but she wasn't mean or cruel. She didn't duck them under or dump them in, she let the kids progress at their own pace. Some of the other children who started lessons around the same time as Daisy were fully confident in the water and were learning the strokes; her little munchkin had yet to put her toe in the pool.

Daisy slammed her face into McKenna's neck and she felt her warm tears on her skin. Nope, she couldn't do this today. She was too tired, too stressed and it was frankly, too much. She'd learned, as a single mother, to choose her battles. There were days when she just couldn't cope by herself and this was one of them. This was a "retreat to fight another time" situation…

McKenna turned around to tell Jed that she was calling it quits, to ask him to take them home. Except that Jed, who'd worn a pained, uncomfortable expression from her house to the pool—listening to Daisy wail was heart wrenching, she admitted—wasn't anywhere to be seen. So much for being their bodyguard. If he was planning on sticking around then he'd have to learn, fast, that life with a three-year-old was not always easy and not always fun.

But, she tightened her hold on Daisy, she wouldn't change a thing. If Zoo had lived and come around to the idea of being a father, would life be easier, would she be sharing these moments with him? Probably, definitely, not, she answered herself, resting her head against Daisy's. Zoo had a short attention span and he hadn't been the type to hang in for the long haul. Booze, drugs, and parties had been his top three priorities; she and Daisy wouldn't have made the list.

It didn't matter, she had to deal with what was and the reality was that she was Daisy's parent and the buck stopped with her. Every single time. Daisy had, thank God, finally stopped screaming and her face, resting on her shoulder, was now turned away from her. Where was Jed? She just wanted to take her girl and go home, was that too much to ask?

"Hey, pretty girl."

McKenna turned around and her mouth fell open. Jed was dressed in swimming shorts and nothing else. His chest, tanned and lightly covered with golden hair, was about an acre wide and the muscles she'd, oh so briefly explored, were clearly defined. She couldn't help her eyes dropping south; yeah, he had an eight pack, narrow hips, and strong thighs covered by those black shorts. God, he even had nice feet.

And a nice package...*lift those eyes up, McKenna Dixon!*

"What are you doing?" she squawked. "Where did you get those shorts from?"

"At the swim shop at the entrance," Jed replied and put his hand on Daisy's back.

"Hey, short stuff," he crooned and McKenna couldn't believe that his deep baritone could sound so tender, so persuasive.

Daisy just looked at him, her thumb in her mouth.

McKenna opened her mouth to speak but Jed's quick frown had her snapping her mouth closed. What was he doing?

"I'm pretty tall, don't you think?"

Daisy nodded and McKenna felt Jed's hand on her hip, moving her closer to the pool. She followed his lead and edged closer to the water. "Want to see where the water comes up to my body? Do you think it'll come up to my head?"

"Maybe," Daisy whispered the words.

Jed looked at the water and then back to Daisy, his face puzzled. "Well, I'm not sure about that."

"It will," Daisy replied, stubborn as always.

"Shall we check?" Jed asked, walking closer to the edge. McKenna felt Daisy tense and then her little hand shot out to touch Jed's bare shoulder.

"It's scary...aren't you scared?" she asked around her thumb.

"I can swim really, really well so if it's that deep then I'll just swim to the wall," Jed told her and McKenna knew that it wasn't a lie. "I'm not scared but it's okay if you are."

"Maybe just a little," Daisy defiantly told him, lifting her face from her shoulder.

McKenna saw amusement flash in his eyes. "That's okay. So was I when I first started to learn. So, do you want to see if the water goes over my head?"

Daisy nodded and Jed just kept his steady, encouraging eyes on her face. "If I do, will you come and sit on the edge of the pool?"

Daisy leaned away from McKenna and bit her bottom lip, her glance going from the water to Jed and back again. "What if I slip?"

"I'll catch you," Jed assured her, his tone low and absolute and McKenna believed him. He wouldn't let anything happen to Daisy and Daisy seemed to realize that, too. "Shall we try?"

Daisy gave him a slow nod. Jed dropped to his haunches, crooked his finger at Daisy, and McKenna lowered her to the floor. Jed whispered in her ear and a small smile touched Daisy's lips. Then she took a couple of steps back from the pool. Dammit, two steps forward and six back. What happened to her sitting on the edge of the pool? What had Jed said to scupper that idea?

Then Jed walked toward the pool, all six-three of easy, fluid masculine grace, bounced on his toes, and rolled into the water, creating a rather large explosion that drenched McKenna from head to toe.

She heard Daisy's whoop of laughter as she spluttered and pushed wet hair out of her face.

"You jerk!" she yelled at Jed, who was standing waist deep in the water, his hands slicking his hair off his face. "I'm soaking you, you…cretin!" she shouted, pulling her shirt away from her breasts. She was wearing a see-through top and a mostly transparent bra and she was pretty sure that he was seeing far more than she wanted him too. "Why did you do that?"

Jed's eyes drifted over her chest and the corners of his mouth kicked up. "Nice. You could easily win a wet T-shirt competition." He held up his hand when she started to splutter with indignation. "That's why I did it."

McKenna looked toward where he gestured and there was her little girl, sitting in the lapping water at the edge of the pool, splashing the warm water on her thighs, over her knees and smiling.

This was more progress than she'd ever made. That, and seeing the hot, naked desire in Jed's eyes as he raked his eyes over her chest, was almost worth getting drenched for.

Almost.

"THANKS FOR ARRANGING Daisy to go to Mattie's so that you could come with me tonight," Jed said, glancing across the interior of the SUV to the passenger seat.

Man, McKenna looked gorgeous. Her dress was a pale blush color, with drapes of fabric that fell from the scoop neckline to mid-thigh. She'd curled her hair and sprayed herself with a deeper, darker scent that made him think of hot nights, the sound of waves slapping a beach, and sun-kissed skin.

He sounded like a girl; he was pretty sure that getting laid would help with that.

"It was the least I could do since you got Daisy into the pool, even if she looked like she was strangling you half the time."

"I did get her to kick her legs," Jed interrupted and hoped that McKenna missed the note of pride in his voice. What was that about? So he'd got a toddler into a pool and to kick her little legs…who cared?

I do.

"I never thought we'd see the day." So did McKenna, obviously. "You were utterly marvelous," McKenna softly said as she turned in her seat to look at him.

"I would've cut off my own right arm if that was what was required to get her to stop crying," Jed muttered. And that wasn't much of an exaggeration. That was a torture that he never wanted to experience again.

"Pretty intense, huh? You should try two nights solid of colicky screaming."

Cut off his arm? Hell, he'd chew it off in those circumstances.

He turned to look at her and his heart bumped at the soft look on her face. He gripped the steering wheel and fought the urge to pull over, telling himself that he wasn't allowed to maul her on a dark, deserted road. Mostly because if he started then there was no way he'd stop. Dammit, it was tempting and he was half-irritated and half-grateful when

McKenna's brisk voice pulled him back to sanity.

"Besides, you said that you wouldn't leave me alone and I wasn't prepared to let you use me as an excuse for you to duck out on seeing your family, to avoid attending."

Jed half smiled at McKenna's observation, liking the fact that she called a spade a shovel. That was exactly what he'd intended to do. Sure, he wanted to meet Leah's fiancé, but he could do that without having to break bread with his father and his trophy wife…and a lot of relatives he hadn't seen for the best part of a decade. He would prefer to sit down on his own with Heath; interrogation was so much easier without an audience. As it was, he had Seth using the computer division of Pytheon to do a deep background check and as soon as he got that intel, he'd know Leah's guy inside out.

God, he really hoped that Heath checked out. He'd failed Leah in so many ways, so many times and he really didn't want to be the bearer of bad news. But there was no way that he'd allow her to get married without having all the facts, without knowing exactly who she was marrying. Knowledge, he believed, was power.

"No comment, huh?" McKenna said from her corner of the car.

Jed shifted down and took the first sharp corner of the long, windy road that would take them to the up market restaurant situated ten minutes out of town and on a bluff with incredible sea views.

"My father and I get along so much better when there is a great deal of distance between us," he said, resting his wrist on the top of the steering wheel. "We get along superbly well when we have no contact at all."

McKenna crossed her legs and rested her head on the corner of her seat. "I'm sorry to hear that. I loved my dad and we were exceptionally close."

"How old were you when he died?"

McKenna's hands smoothed the fabric of her dress over her thigh. "Eighteen. My world fell apart. It had been him and me for so long—my mom died when I was two so I don't remember her—but my dad and I were tight."

He heard the pain in her voice and he could empathize. He'd been older when his mom passed on but he could relate. It felt like the foundations of life cracking and it wasn't something easily recovered from. "How did you—" Jed cleared his throat "—handle it?"

He heard McKenna's low sigh. "Badly," she admitted. "I did what every lost, rich, pain-filled princess does when she's hurting…I acted out. I tried to fill the hole and chase the pain away by partying too much and too hard, shopping excessively, dating constantly. I bounced from bad man to bad man—all crazy and all unavailable—party to party, hangover to hangover."

Jed grimaced. He knew how it felt to be lost and alone. "What changed?"

"I fell."

Jed flicked her a quick glance and saw the soft, smile on her face. "Fell?"

"Fell in love, properly and completely, when I got pregnant with Daisy." McKenna straightened in her seat and turned to stare out of the window so he could only see half her profile.

"So what did the police officer have to say?" McKenna asked, referring to the visit from the same policeman who had arrived on her doorstep around six.

She'd left Jed to talk to him as Daisy, exhausted and whiny, had interrupted the conversation every time McKenna took her attention off her. Jed got the impression she was grateful that, for once, she could share the load. Raising a child on your own, he was quickly realizing, was tougher than SAS school and twice as tiring.

"Apparently Craig Daniels is alibi-ed five times over for the time that your house was broken into. He's shocked and saddened that you think that he could be your stalker. He insinuated that you are delusional and an attention-seeker."

"Bastard," McKenna muttered.

"Have you ever seen him driving past? Hanging around your house?"

"My house is on one of the main roads of Simons Town, Jed. Of course I've seen him, he slows down and creeps past but I can't stop him from using the road; thousands do."

Jed rubbed the back of his neck, frustrated. "What I don't understand is why he suddenly escalated from emails and phone calls to breaking and entering. What was the trigger?"

McKenna shrugged. "Haven't a clue." She held her hand parallel to her thigh and Jed noticed the tremors in her fingers. "My hands shake, all the time. I just want him to stop, Jed. I'm trying to act as normal as possible but underneath I feel terrified. I keep looking over my shoulder and I feel like there's a ghost in my life, someone watching and waiting for the perfect time to strike."

He did, too. The thought of her being the crosshairs of this sick cretin made the bile rise up in his throat. Maybe he should pay Daniels a visit and give him a taste of his own medicine. A little pain, a little pressure, lots of threats. And he had the right skills to do it in such a way that he'd never be caught and, better, never identified.

It was something to think about. Time to take the shadows out of her eyes, Jed decided. She deserved a night off where she didn't have to think about stalkers or dangers or threats. He wasn't the best conversationalist in the world but he knew that every mother loved talking about her kid. Thinking of the way that Daisy happily went to Mattie when they dropped her off earlier, he said: "Daisy is really comfortable with Mattie, isn't she?"

"For all intents and purposed, Mattie is her second mother."

"Have you always been close?"

He saw the shake of her head. "Only in the last couple of years. Our fathers were very different and we didn't have much contact growing up."

"Different how?"

"Her father is very religious and terribly conservative; actually, so is Mattie, believe it or not. My father was the exact opposite. He was a rebel and alternative and marched to the beat of his own drum. Irreverent, brilliant, outspoken, anti-establishment. Anti-religion. He was such a charismatic, exciting man," McKenna said, her tone sad and wistful. "Mattie's father thought he led a life of sin and refused to acknowledge him and, because I have a baby out of wedlock, he pretty much ignores Daisy and me, too. Mattie and I only reconnected after my dad passed."

McKenna fiddled with the small clutch bag in her lap. "Mattie is fantastic with Daisy and I love her…she's family."

Jed could relate to that. He loved Leah, desperately, but hated the fact that she was getting married. As for his father, he just hated him. Simple, really.

"How did you get into designing wedding dresses?"

McKenna smiled at his question. "A friend couldn't find a wedding dress she liked so I sat down with her and started playing with designs to see if I could nail what she wanted. I did and then she wanted me to make the dress but I'm not a seamstress. I knew that Mattie loved to sew and was meticulous at it. I designed the dress, she made it and a business was born."

"And she just moved across the world, just like that?" Jed asked as they approached the turn off that led to the country house and restaurant.

"I was a single mom with no support structure and, because she's nuts about babies and kids, she offered to help me," McKenna explained.

"In time or with money?"

"I have a trust fund and support from Daisy's father's family so money wasn't the problem. But you don't realize how draining it can be raising a child on your own, especially one with colic. She came, stayed, and I will always love her for that. She saved me."

Jed could feel the eyes on his face and turned his head to see her frowning. "What?" he demanded.

"You didn't ask me how much my trust fund was worth." McKenna tipped her head to one side.

Jed rolled his eyes. People were, frequently as it turned out, stupid. And rude. "I don't care how much money you have, it's not important," he replied, his voice cool. "Do people *really* ask you that?"

"Yes, Craig did. He just came out and demanded the figure," McKenna said, contempt in her voice. "You really don't care?"

"As much as I care about nail polish and reality TV," Jed assured her and was rewarded with her low, sexy laugh.

The car cut through the inky darkness and in the distance he could see the oily blackness of the Atlantic Ocean. The moon was hidden behind low clouds and above them he could see the flickering lights of the country house that held the restaurant they were headed to. He'd spoken the truth, if she had five hundred or five billion dollars, the money was inconsequential. There were other things he'd like to know though, reluctantly admitting that he was tempted to dig deeper. He wanted to know about Daisy's father, why McKenna was still single and determined to stay that way, to hear about those lonely nights, her fears, how she felt about being a young single mother.

But he didn't have the right to ask her about any of that; he wasn't in a position to do anything with the information. He couldn't allow himself to get close to her, to hear her story and then bail. That wasn't fair on her, or on him.

Rolling stones gathered no moss…or any friends either. Generally, he was okay with that, but tonight? Not so much.

Jed swung into the driveway and parked in the designated area. In the dark space of his vehicle he could smell McKenna's teasing scent, could feel the heat of her look, wanted to touch the ocean of creaminess that was her skin. With her hair pinned up onto her head in a messy style that looked fantastic and her smoky eyes, she looked so damn sexy that his breath caught in his throat.

"Don't look at me like that," McKenna whispered, breaking their sexually laden stare.

"I can't help it," Jed muttered, clenching his fist to keep from reaching for her.

"When you look at me, like that, its feels like I can't breathe. I feel like I need oxygen."

That and hot, slow sex, Jed agreed. Sighing, he pulled himself together, opened his door, and climbed out of the car. Grabbing his jacket, he slipped it on before slamming the door closed and walking around the car to open McKenna's door.

McKenna refused to meet his eyes as she placed her hand in his to climb down from the high car. When she was steady on those ridiculously high heels, he lifted her chin with the knuckle of his index finger. "I need you, Mac."

McKenna's eyes widened. "How?"

Jed's brows pulled together. "In my bed, sexually. Why, what did you think I meant?"

McKenna looked him dead in the eye and lifted her

shoulders. “Just making sure that you weren’t implying that you wanted something more than, well, sex.”

“And you would have a problem with that?”

McKenna nodded and looked sad. “Hell, yes. I don’t play any games that involve the heart anymore.”

Good. He didn’t play heart games either. He didn’t think he even had a heart. So whatever this craziness was that was happening between him and McKenna was just sexual, just lust. Good, he could handle lust and desire.

So why, he wondered, as he followed her to the front door of the ornate, brightly lit house, wasn’t he feeling more relieved and instead, having trouble convincing himself?

Chapter Seven

"WHY DID YOU leave the army, Jed?"

Beside her, McKenna felt Jed tense and knew that the question, asked by an elderly Hamilton aunt seated opposite them, annoyed him. He tapped his finger against his glass and frowned.

"The life expectancy isn't good," he replied.

McKenna winced at his cold, flat don't-pursue-this answer but his aunt, bless her, wasn't discouraged. "And photography? Isn't that a rather...unstable career? Does your father approve of you traveling the world snapping pictures?"

Unfortunately her question dropped into one of those spaces when the entire table was silent and eleven heads swiveled in their direction. McKenna watched as Jed and his father locked eyes and was reminded of a nature program she'd recently watched with Daisy. Jed and his father were two buffalo bulls, one young, one older, both powerful. Both determined to win.

A cold smile, borrowed she was sure from a great white shark, pulled up the corners of the general's mouth. "Jed doesn't care whether I approve or not. He doesn't have an ounce of respect for me, as a father or as a soldier."

"Certainly not as a husband," Jed muttered, his voice so

low that only McKenna caught his words.

"You taught us that it was rude to disagree with our elders so I won't," Jed raised his voice but his tone remained cool and free of emotion.

Note to self: do not piss Jed off, McKenna told herself.

"I also taught you to honor traditions and to serve your country," Thaddius snapped.

"I did," Jed calmly said but McKenna felt the slight bouncing of his knee next to hers.

She placed her hand on his thigh and squeezed and he immediately stilled. His hand covered hers and she suspected he didn't know that his grip on her fingers was tighter than she liked.

"Stop it you two," Leah ordered as her guests did the tennis movement, head and eyes flicking from one end of the table to the next, waiting to see who would score the winning shot. "This is my engagement party so behave!"

"Yes, Jed, you are being inexcusably rude."

McKenna narrowed her eyes at the general's wife, Angela. There was nothing angelic in those calculating eyes, in the frankly appreciative and sultry looks she'd been sending Jed all evening. McKenna's female intuition told her that Angela chastising Jed had nothing to do with her siding with her husband and everything to do with the fact that Jed had deliberately ignored her, and her impressive cleavage, all evening.

Jed's smile held no amusement as he looked at his father's trophy wife. "Luckily, I care as much for your opinion, Angela, as I do for his."

It took a while for Jed's words to sink in and when they did, Angela pouted and turned to her husband. "Thad!"

McKenna rolled her eyes, annoyed. She had no patience with women who poked the bear and then squealed when the beast bared his teeth. And, judging by all the animal references, she really should stop watching nature programs with Daisy.

"Apologize to my wife!" Thaddius roared.

Eyes widened and mouths dropped open but Jed, looking weary, just shook his head and pushed his chair back to stand up. His face was a blank mask but, looking up, McKenna could see only a hint of frustration in his eyes. He was a hell of an actor, McKenna admitted.

He managed to send her a tiny smile and when he spoke, she had to strain to hear his words. "As I said, we need continents between us."

Thaddius picked up his tumbler and held it loosely in his hands. "You are such a disappointment to me, Jed."

"Dad!" Leah objected, throwing her hands up in the air.

"Yeah, I realized that a long, long time ago, Thaddius." Jed looked down at her and placed his hand on her shoulder. "I need some air. Stay put, okay?"

McKenna reached up to squeeze his fingers. "Want me to come with you?" she asked, in a low whisper, prepared to follow him wherever he wanted to go.

"Nah, I've got this," Jed replied, spinning around to walk toward the floor to ceiling doors that led onto the terrace of the restaurant.

McKenna didn't blame him for needing to take a break.

She watched him as he made his way through the tables of the crowded restaurant toward the double doors that led to the terrace that ran along the length of the building. His gait looked relaxed but McKenna noticed the tension in his neck, his hunched shoulders. She took a large gulp of her wine and looked at the half full glass that Jed had left behind. Because he was driving, he couldn't drink, and if there was ever a social function that required alcohol, then Leah's—poor, poor girl—engagement dinner was it.

McKenna looked at Thaddius and tipped her head, watching him as he talked to Leah's fiancé. Jed had to be his mother's child, she mused. He didn't look anything like his shorter, stouter father and, while she was sure they were equally stubborn and determined, Jed's ego wasn't half the size of his father's. He was a strong man but knew how to harness his strength, both mental and physical. He was fully in control of his actions and reactions and, after dealing with Darren and Zoo who acted first and thought later—sometimes much later—she found that quality ridiculously attractive.

McKenna looked at Leah and raised her eyebrows. Leah nodded once, slowly. *Go to him,* her expression suggested, *he needs…someone.* Not sure if that someone was her, McKenna held Leah's eye but Jed's sister's face remained beseeching, so McKenna pushed her chair back, murmured a soft excuse and followed Jed's path through the tables.

The terrace was full of shadows and dark corners and the air was crisp thanks to the mist that was rolling off the ocean. McKenna wrapped her hands around the wooden balustrade and looked down to see vicious waves crashing onto the rocky shoreline below. The moon played peek-a-boo with the clouds and McKenna rested her forearms on the wood and waited for Jed to approach her. He was at the far end of the terrace, watching her…she could feel his gaze touching the line of her back, wandering over her rounded bottom and down her legs.

She didn't hear him coming—how could such a big man walk so quietly?—and she sucked in her breath when a hot, masculine finger slid up the bare skin on the back of her thigh.

"If someone had to walk out right now you'd give them a hell of a show," Jed said, scraping his knuckles on the underside of her right butt cheek. "You absolutely can't bend over in that dress," he added as he stepped up to the balustrade to stand beside her. "But I have to say that that I'm a sucker for tiny thongs."

McKenna knew that nobody from the restaurant could see her, she had walked down the terrace and they were standing in complete darkness. It was a perfect place for some naughtiness, for stolen touches and illicit kisses. McKenna looked at Jed's hard, remote profile and thought if there was ever a man in need of a distraction, this man was it. Talking would get her nowhere; she just knew he wouldn't discuss his family and his relationship with his father. He would dismiss her attempts at comfort…she'd just be wasting her time.

But distract him. *That* she could do. With one kiss she could make him forget that brief but ugly exchange with his father. And it wasn't all altruistic, she wanted to kiss him, she'd wanted those hot, hard hands on her, that mouth covering hers…

Jed turned his head and his face softened as he looked at her. One corner of his mouth kicked up and he raised an eyebrow. "You going to kiss and make it better?" he asked, reading her mind.

McKenna was about to respond with a smart aleck comment but the sharp words died in her throat. Instead she just nodded once, quickly. "If that's what you want."

He walked quietly but he could move quickly, McKenna realized when hot hands landed on her hips and his fingertips dug into her skin, yanking her against him, hot and already hard.

"It's what I need," he stated as one hand moved up her body to hold the back of her head as his mouth touched hers. She expected…*hell*, she didn't know what she expected McKenna admitted as those clever, sensuous lips met hers. Instead of wild and hard, a little crazy, his kiss was exploratory, sexy, a little sweet. McKenna lifted her hands to place them on his pecs, feeling hard muscle under her hands and she sighed into his mouth, her lips slipping open to allow a puff of air to escape. Jed's tongue slipped inside, touched hers, and the spark ignited a fireball of complete crazy. She dropped her hands, pressed her breasts into his chest and her hips slammed into his, pushing her stomach into his erection.

As their kiss became a duel for control, their hands darted from body part to body part, searching for skin. McKenna pulled Jed's shirt out of his pants to run her hands over his broad back, across his rock-hard stomach. Her hand dropped and, through the barrier of his trousers, she flirted with the tip of his shaft. Jed's hands snuck under her dress, skimmed the back of her thighs and cupped her bare buttocks, lifting her higher against him so that her mound was riding his cock. She groaned and tilted her hips so that she could hit the spot and when she did she froze with pleasure. To hell with him needing this, *she* needed this. She needed to feel like a woman again, needed to feel lost in a man's touch, wet from his kisses and crazy with the need to have him inside her, filling her.

"Want you, want you, want you," McKenna chanted, her hands going to the front of his pants, circling as much of his erection as his pants allowed.

Jed swore, resting his forehead against hers. "We have to slow down. We can't do this here."

McKenna didn't care. "It's dark. No one is looking."

Jed groaned as he pulled her hand off his dick. "McKenna, we can't. Not. Here."

She barely registered the words but the fact that he was stepping away from her, retreating, finally penetrated her sexual haze. Dear Lord, she thought as he tucked his shirt back into his pants, she'd been half a minute and one kiss away from letting him slide on home. Who was this person she turned into when she was with him? How did he do that?

She fell apart in his arms and her skin was still buzzing. Thank God the roaring in her ears started to subside. Her little scrap of material that made up her thong was soaked and her nipples were aching, feeling confined by the fabric of her strapless bra. Jed, she could see from the corner of her eye, just looked like he was standing in line waiting to order coffee.

No prizes for guessing who never had a problem getting laid, who could take and leave sex, who wasn't a churning, electrified mess of hormones. And there would certainly be no prizes for guessing who was so damn horny—and now properly, comprehensively mortified—that she was prepared to get jiggy on a darkened terrace twenty feet from a room full of Simons Town's elite. She felt ambushed, decimated by this intense, enthralling connection with this man, someone who was little more than a stranger. Kissing Jed was the most intense high she'd ever experienced and had she really begged him to nail her in a semi-public place?

Good grief.

Could she do this…could she sleep with him and keep it simple? She wanted to convince herself that she could and blithely tell herself that she could keep it light and sexy, that she'd keep all the messy emotions out of it. But…she sighed…but she didn't have the best track record when it came to dealing with these high octane men and the chemistry they generated. She'd had a powerful connection with Darren, and she'd loved him with an intensity that still, even in hindsight, scared her. When he moved on, after everything she'd given him, it felt like every fairy and butterfly in the world died.

When Zoo, bold and artistic, walked up to her in a club

and boldly, and expertly, kissed her, she'd fallen at his feet. Lightning didn't strike the same object twice, nothing would go wrong. She would be fine, she could handle the temperamental, moody, and demanding man; but he just had to kiss her and she'd give him anything, do anything. Hell, she would've helped Zoo move bodies, he'd been that enthralling, that addictive. But her brain kicked into another gear when she got pregnant and his demand that she have an abortion flipped a switch for her. She realized that while he was an exciting boyfriend, he would be a bad, neglectful father and a terrible husband or partner. He had been arrogant, selfish and irresponsible, and totally self-absorbed. Yet she'd loved him and she'd mourned him. It was never supposed to end that way.

But with Jed, something more than chemistry was happening and she didn't like it. Her body was screaming for sex but her mind was insisting that sleeping with him would be taking the first step down a very slippery slope. He was too attractive and this time she wasn't talking about his solid body and sexy face. No, she liked his razor-sharp mind, the protective streak he refused to admit he had, the way he jumped into a pool to encourage her daughter to swim. She liked the ways his eyes sharpened when something caught his interest, his dry sense of humor, and his calm, stable presence. He was strong and smart and protective…both of her and her child.

She felt safe and that raised another issue. Was she confusing gratitude with attraction? Did she want to fall into his embrace because for the first time in forever she felt like she had someone who had her back? Mentally and physically. When you'd been alone for a long time, company, and sexy company at that, had the ability to turn a girl's head.

Sensible McKenna knew how this path ended, every time she walked it she ended up at the bottom of a cliff. Clever McKenna knew that sleeping with him was a very bad idea.

Desperate-to-sleep-with-Jed, horny McKenna didn't care.

"Jed."

Saved by the crabby general, McKenna mused.

Jed cursed and slowly turned around, his arm shooting out to pull McKenna to his side. Interesting that he felt the need to protect her against his father, McKenna mused. She kept her eyes on Jed's face, intrigued by the way his body straightened and tensed. If she didn't know better, she would assume that he was still a highly trained soldier; he looked alert, focused, and like he was anticipating trouble.

"Not a good time, Thaddius," Jed said in a hard, cold tone.

Thaddius ignored him and clasped his hands behind his back. "I don't appreciate you insulting my wife and ignoring us for the best part of the evening."

"Well, I didn't appreciate the fact that you had an affair with her while my mother lay dying of cancer," Jed replied, his words low and slow and as cold as an Arctic snowstorm.

Whoa. McKenna tried to walk away but Jed's arm around her waist just tightened and she stayed where she was, still feeling like she was standing between the devil and the deep blue sea. She didn't think she should be hearing this.

"That was no reason to give up your career in the Special Forces. Hamiltons serve, dammit!"

"Don't you dare start spouting your crap about honor and service and respect. Your words mean nothing to me because none of those values extended to your family, especially to your wife. Do you remember her? She was the one who used to drop in and out of consciousness, always calling your name. And where were you? Screwing Miss September?" Jed pushed a hand through his hair before gripping the bridge of his nose with his thumb and forefinger. "I'm not having this argument, not again." He flicked her a quick, hard look and jerked his head. "Let's go."

McKenna nodded and placed her hand on the one gripping her waist, squeezing his fingers to show her support. She saw a quick, tiny hitch of his mouth and knew that it was his way of saying he appreciated the gesture. Then Jed was walking her across the terrace and she practically had to skip to keep up with his long stride as they crossed the stone floor.

"I know what you are up to, Jed."

Jed stopped so abruptly that McKenna nearly tripped over her feet. He steadied her before turning to look at Thaddius.

He looked hard and dangerous and….my, so sexy. "What, exactly, do you mean by that?"

"It means that I was a high ranking officer in the most powerful army in the world. Did you honestly think I wouldn't find out?"

Again, she kept her eyes on Jed and she caught the tiny flick of tension in his jaw, the infinitesimal narrowing of his eyes. His father had hit a very big nerve.

"I have no idea what you're talking about," Jed said, his voice calm and even and he sounded, genuinely, puzzled. But, on an instinctive level, McKenna knew that he was lying through his very white teeth.

Thaddius looked past them to where Leah and Heath were sitting at the table and McKenna looked to where he nodded. Leah was laughing, looking happy, but Heath had his eyes trained on them, his gaze assessing and vaguely amused. He suddenly looked nothing like the mild mannered man she'd assumed him to be.

"I'm just a photographer, Thaddius."

"Yeah, sure." Thaddius nodded, his face blatantly skeptical. He turned his eyes back to Jed and his expression was fierce and McKenna could instantly see why he'd risen so far and so fast.

"I've done my own digging but he checks out. If you find out anything, you let me know."

"*If* I was in a position to find out anything," Jed slowly responded, "I'd handle the situation myself."

Huh? Say what? Thaddius seemed to understand because he nodded once, brushed past them, and strode back to the table, taking his place next to his wife.

Jed dropped his arm, rolled his head on his shoulders, and grimaced. "My father, always a pleasure."

McKenna folded her arms and tapped her foot. She knew she had virtually no chance of eliciting any information from him but she thought that she'd give it a whirl. "So what, exactly, are you up to?"

Jed gripped the back of her neck and dropped a swift kiss on her mouth. "All I am up to is trying to convince you to go to bed with me."

McKenna ignored his words and sent him a narrow eyed look. "It's scary how well you lie, Hamilton." When he just gave her that slightly puzzled look she threw her hands up into the air.

"I'm a photographer, Mac. That's it."

McKenna shook her head. "No, that's not it." She sighed her disappointment. "I'd far prefer to be hurt by the truth than comforted by a lie, Jed. Every time. You don't have to tell me but don't lie to me, okay?"

Jed moved his gaze to a point past her head and, for the first time, she saw the emotions running wild across his face. Regret, surprise, a hint of relief. He eventually looked down at her and sent her a rueful smile. "I'm not lying. But, yeah, you're half-right. I can't tell you what I do but yeah, photography isn't *all* that I do."

It was a huge concession, McKenna realized. *Photography isn't all that I do...* six words that implied a measure of trust.

She had to ask one more burning question. "Is it dangerous?"

Jed didn't answer her straight away. "Some of the places I travel to are dangerous, but I keep my lens straight and my nose clean."

McKenna wasn't about to let him get away with that evasion. "I wasn't talking about your photography, Jed; I'm asking whether whatever else you do has the element of danger."

Jed touched her cheek with his fingertips before abruptly dropping his hand. He nodded sharply. "Sometimes."

McKenna made herself smile at him, wishing that she could take the question back. The thought of Jed getting hurt, or killed, made her blood freeze. She hauled in a breath, counted to ten, and slowly expelled the air, trying to stop her heart from exploding. She was just being overly dramatic, too imaginative for words.

"Can you talk about what you do? Even a little?"

Since her question was more hope than expectation, McKenna wasn't surprised by his firm, unequivocal "No."

She forced another smile. "Don't do anything stupid, 'kay?"

"I'll try not to," Jed gravely replied but she could see amusement in his eyes. "Let's go home, Mac."

McKenna nodded. "Yeah, let's do that."

Chapter Eight

AT THE KITCHEN door, Jed took the keys from McKenna's hand and opened the door, placing his hand low on her back to push her and Daisy inside. As soon as she stepped into her kitchen, McKenna slipped out of her shoes, sighing as she adjusted a sleeping Daisy on her hip. They'd picked her up from Mattie's house and she just wanted to get Daisy in her own bed and climb into bed herself…preferably with Jed. Oh, she'd given up trying to talk herself out of sleeping with him; they both knew that it was going to happen. They'd said little on the drive home but Jed's hand, high up on her thigh, under her dress—his thumb rhythmically and deliciously stroking her bare skin, made silent promises.

McKenna licked her lips as heat pooled in her womb and wondered how it would start. After she put Daisy to bed, should she find him or would he find her? Would he come to her room? Did she want it hot and fast, slow and sweet? Should she change, slip into something sexier—did she have something sexy to slip into? She definitely wanted to brush her teeth, McKenna decided as she started to walk across room to the hallway and she walked straight into Jed's outstretched arm.

"What the hell are you doing?" he demanded, in a hushed whisper.

McKenna looked down at his arm and back to his frowning face. Okay, that wasn't the look of a man who was desperate to get her naked and panting. "Putting my daughter to bed."

"Civilians." Jed looked exasperated. "We've been out all night; I'd like to check the place out to make sure that we have no unwanted guests before you go upstairs. Is that okay with you?"

McKenna lifted her chin. "There is no need to get snotty."

"Honey, I've dealt with my father, what felt like a million curious relations, and still haven't managed to have a decent conversation with Leah's man." Jed bent his legs so that he could look her direct in the eye. "I am horny and frustrated and have the biggest set of blue balls in history. I have minimal patience for stupidity right now. You are being threatened, you don't have an alarm—something that will be rectified—so you are going to stay right where you are while I secure the building."

"You could've just explained that," McKenna muttered.

"You're lucky you got that much," Jed retorted.

As he walked away she noticed that he was holding a big, matte black gun against his leg; gripping it as if it were an extension of his hand or arm. Deadly and dangerous, just like its owner.

"You'd better lock that thing away when Daisy is around," McKenna told him when he returned to the kitchen, gesturing to his gun nestled in the small of his back.

"If Daisy, or you, ever lays a hand on my weapon then you can safely assume that I'm dead," Jed told her. He gestured to Daisy, who she'd shifted to her other hip. "Want me to carry her?"

McKenna nodded and Jed gently removed her from her arms. Daisy immediately wrapped her tiny arms around his neck and snuggled down. "She's so light," he marveled, his big hand spanning her back.

"She's grown a lot," McKenna told him, ignoring the lump in her throat. "After a while she becomes a dead weight." She cleared her throat. "If you can just put her on her bed for me, I'll come tuck her in." McKenna looked at her answering machine and saw that there were four missed calls. They were probably all from her stalker and while she knew she should listen to them, then label and store the tape as future evidence, she didn't want to, not tonight. But part of being a grown-up was delaying gratification, doing things she didn't want to do. "I'll just listen to these."

Jed's hand on hers stopped her from pushing the play button. "Don't," he softly said.

McKenna stared at the red four on the display. "I should. And I should check my computer too because the email messages always accompany the phone calls. The police told me to keep a log, to build up the evidence."

Jed held her hand in his, his other arm easily holding Daisy. "Let me do it. I'll listen to them and check the messages on your computer. You put your daughter to bed and snuggle for a while. Be normal and let me do this for you."

She could've argued with him, she could've told him that this was her problem and that she needed to deal with it, but it had been so long since she'd had someone to lean on, someone to share the burden, so she caved without an argument. In the morning she'd be strong again, she'd deal with the mess of her life but tonight she was going to lean…just a little.

He sent her a piercing look before casually asking, "You okay with me looking at your inbox?"

"Sure." McKenna nodded. "I'm a mommy and I sell wedding dresses, that's the sum total of my boring life. There's a folder in the inbox to put any messages I receive from him…you know, keeping a record?"

"Honey, you are anything but boring." Jed brushed her cheek with the back of his fingers. "Put Daze to bed, relax a bit, and come back downstairs. There's a bottle of red in the rack that has our name on it."

Wine and a little conversation would make the journey to bed a little smoother, she thought, touched. She nodded, stood on her toes to kiss the side of his face. "I'll be back soon."

"No rush," Jed's gaze started at her toes and burned a path up her body to her face. "We have all night, Mac. And I intend to take my time."

McKenna wasn't sure if that was a threat or a promise.

JED LOGGED OUT of McKenna's computer, leaned back in her chair, and stared at the empty screen, anger and unease rolling like black waves through his stomach. There were more than a few messages in her inbox and most of them stuck to the same theme—*you think you are so special, someday karma is going to catch up with you, you're a bitch.* Not pleasant but not particularly frightening either. But the messages over the last week or so were another story. The threats were more direct—*I'd love to see you black and blue, you'd look great with your face slashed up, Daisy doesn't deserve a mother like you. Don't think the photographer can protect you from me.*

Well, hell, yes I can! Try me and see.

The new messages also suggested that his presence in the house had escalated the situation and, as a result, he needed to become more vigilant, more alert, and a great deal more cautious. The tone of the letters lifted the hair on the back of his neck and his gut instinct was telling him this went deeper than the pissed off ex of a client. This was darker, older… *and familiar.* His conclusions were unscientific, he admitted, but there was something about the phrasing of the words that suggested knowledge of McKenna. It wasn't sexual but it was deeply personal.

Intense. Extreme. Building…swelling.

On the other hand, if this was Daniels as everyone assumed, then maybe McKenna had pushed a very big button when she'd mentioned his name to the police and his embarrassment could easily be the reason why his harassment had escalated into dark, malevolent threats. Men like Daniels didn't just stop or call it quits, their egos wouldn't allow a woman to get the better of them, to win.

He wasn't going to stop until he chose to and he'd stop on his terms, not McKenna's.

Jed pulled out his mobile and tapped in a number, waiting impatiently for Seth to answer. In the past ten years, he'd never asked for a personal favor and in the past week he'd asked for two. He was in Seth's debt but he could live with it. He needed to know what sort of man was marrying his sister and he needed to make sure that McKenna and Daisy were safe. That simple.

And that complicated.

"You're supposed to be on holiday," Seth complained, sounding, uncharacteristically, flustered. "What?"

"I need a favor—"

"Another one? We haven't even gotten started on the first yet."

Jed raised his eyebrows; that was unusual for the very efficient organization. "I need you to trace some emails and the origins of some phone calls."

"For?" Seth barked.

"A friend…I think she's in danger," Jed reluctantly admitted. "She's been stalked and I don't like the situation."

Seth sighed. "The heiress?" Jed waited through his silence, hearing the chaos emanating from the control room. He heard the click of Seth's fingers flying across his battered keyboard. "You've moved in?" he asked.

Dammit. He hated the fact that Seth could track him. "Yeah."

"You doing her?"

Jed wanted to reach into the phone and place his big hand around the man's big neck but knew that it was a valid question, even if it was crudely put. Emotions interfered with performance, attraction clouded reasoning. He knew this. He didn't like it.

"No," he said between gritted teeth. Well, it was still the truth.

"Keep it that way. Sex is a distraction and distraction can mean the difference between life and death," Seth snapped.

Jed thought about arguing but before he could speak, he heard a roar in the background quickly followed by Seth's curse. Yeah, something big was going down. He felt that familiar kick of excitement, of adrenalin.

"What's happening?" he demanded.

"A little standoff between the ATF and a white supremacy group in Northern California. A client's daughter is with them, she's the leader's second or third wife. His father was born in Kenya and he has links to that country. If they get away, we think he's going to try and leave the country. If he does he'll head there and we're going to need you to track them and her," Seth quickly explained. "You and Bryn are my closest agents, geographically."

"I'm on leave remember?" It was petty but Jed couldn't resist the dig.

"Nobody is on leave when shit goes down," Seth retorted.

Solid truth. Jed pulled his attention back to the problem at hand. "We can't do anything if the wife is an adult," Jed murmured, mostly to himself.

"She's fourteen."

Crap. Jed grabbed a notepad and a pen, about to take down the salient details when he remembered that he was sitting at McKenna's desk, in her house. Leaving here would mean leaving her, and Daisy, vulnerable and there was no way he'd let that happen. If anything happened to her…Jed felt those dark waves crash in his stomach and he shuddered. No, he couldn't—wouldn't, dammit—let that happen. Not to her and not to Daisy. It simply wasn't an option. Ever.

The sane course of action would be to sit down with her and suggest that she contact an organization who specialized in close protection and also to contact a private investigator to figure out who had it in for his—*the*—Dixon girls, and why. That would be the smart, sensible option but there was no way that he was walking away from her, that he would allow anyone else to keep her safe. Nobody would be as paranoid as him, as alert to danger as he would be…

He wasn't going anywhere.

"Bryn will have to handle it," he told Seth. "I'm not moving until this situation with Mac is resolved."

"I could just fire you, you know."

Like that was going to happen. "Yeah, right. So, are you going to help me with the background check or not?"

Of course Seth would, he was his best mate but their relationship dictated that he had to bust his balls first.

"Send me what you want although I have to warn you that it's going to the bottom of the list as we have a couple of situations here that are infinitely more important."

"Not to me."

Seth waited a beat before speaking again. "We have good reasons why we do not allow fraternization between our operatives and our clients, Jed. Lines get blurred which lead to mistakes. Don't do anything you're going to regret, bud," Seth added before disconnecting.

Yeah, it would be wiser to step back, to keep his distance. He was over thinking this, falling for the hearth and happy home vibe happening in this house. It didn't mean anything; it couldn't mean anything. He wasn't a happy home and hearth type of guy. He needed to concentrate on protecting her and stop thinking about what she would feel like, taste like. But he could have one night, couldn't he? One crazy, hot, sexy night so that he could stop wondering, stop fantasizing. It was unlikely that Daniels would break into the house with him there. He was the type to ambush McKenna when she was alone and if he did, Jed would hear him. He had ears like a bat and a sixth sense for trouble.

One night and they'd be fine. One night and they could go back to normal…

Whatever the hell that was. And then he heard a thump…

MCKENNA, PULLED FROM a doze, opened her eyes, suddenly and instantly awake. She'd heard something, struggling to identify the sound that penetrated her light sleep. She knew this house, knew its rattles and shudders, knew the sound of the wind as it swirled overhead, the creak of the stairs. She was sitting in the rocking chair in Daisy's room and Daisy was curled up against her chest, fast asleep. She'd woken up soon after Jed put her into bed and McKenna, knowing that the quickest way to get her to go back to sleep so that she could go downstairs, had decided to rock her as she'd done when Daisy was a baby. In the process she'd rocked herself to sleep as well.

McKenna gasped when a figure stepped into the room and she called herself an idiot when she realized that it was Jed. He walked over to them and placed a hand on Daisy's back.

"So you heard it too?" she asked, looking up at him. "What was it?"

"Not sure." Jed shrugged. "I heard some scraping, a quick bang. I've taken a look around and I'm not sure what made the noise but there's nobody out there."

McKenna frowned, a little put out. "Oh…I thought you would've checked on us before you went on your little recon."

Jed smiled. His smiles, McKenna realized, were coming a lot quicker and were a lot brighter than before. "I did. This is my second check. You made it easier by being together."

Aw. There was no chance of resisting this amazing man, especially since he looked so sexy with his creased, open dress shirt, shadowed jaw, holding his big gun down the side of his leg.

McKenna dragged her eyes off Jed's washboard abs and looked at her sleeping child. "Sorry, I fell asleep. I must have been more tired than I thought."

"No worries, I was longer than I thought I'd be."

"What did you find on the computer?" McKenna asked as Jed placed his gun on a tall shelf so that he could lift Daisy off her lap.

Jed flicked her a glance before gently placing Daisy between the covers in her bed.

"No more about that tonight, Legs," Jed told her in a hoarse voice, brushing past her to pick up his gun.

She followed him into the hallway outside. She stepped out of the doorway and in the low light of Daisy's night-light, noticed his blazing eyes and, dropping her eyes south, the tent in his pants his erection made. He didn't look embarrassed by his display of desire. He just stood there, tall and proud, waiting for her to make the next move.

He wouldn't ask again, he wouldn't push her for more. He was just showing her that he wanted her, no words were necessary. She licked her lips and ran her foot over the hallway runner.

"For how long?" she asked, her mouth super dry.

He knew what she was asking without her having to articulate the words. Jed didn't drop his eyes from hers. "Tonight…a couple of hours, that's it. Tomorrow I ramp up your protection and I can't afford to be distracted by thoughts of wondering how you taste, feel, what it feels like to be inside you."

McKenna's eyes widened. "You've been thinking that? Since when?"

Jed released a low laugh. "Oh, since a millisecond after I

first laid eyes on you."

"Me too," McKenna reluctantly admitted, sucking in her bottom lip. "A couple of hours? Then we go back to normal?"

"Not that we have any idea what normal actually is," she added.

Jed didn't smile; he just stood looking tall and sexy and utterly, comprehensively male. McKenna felt her womb tighten, her nipples puckered in anticipation and wondered how this would start, how this would happen. The world around her disappeared, it was just her and Jed and the crackle of electricity between them. She was counting to ten and if he didn't do something—anything!—besides looking at her like she was the decadent icing on a luxurious chocolate cake, she was going to jump him.

Nine, eight, seven, six…

"I'm going to make you scream," Jed promised her and she believed him.

Five, four, three…

"Bedroom," Jed ordered and McKenna couldn't find the energy to object to his abrupt command.

After all, it was exactly where she wanted to be. She walked across the hallway, pushed open the door to her room and walked inside. Jed was a half-step behind her but he walked past her to the side table and checked his weapon before sliding it into the bedside table drawer. His attention was now fully on her and she swallowed nervously as he moved toward her, his feet silent on the wooden floors. The drumming of her heartbeat increased as he approached and, to McKenna, it seemed loud enough to wake Daisy. And the neighbors. Her body sighed when long hands reached out to grab her hips and pull her into that place where she most wanted to be. Her breasts flattened against the immovable wall of his chest and she could feel the rasp of his chest hair through the thin fabric of her dress. Then Jed's mouth covered hers and he was there, with her, tongue touching hers, bodies aligned and the world briefly made sense before it disappeared.

Something hot and wild and deeper than attraction flared between them as McKenna succumbed to the magic of his mouth. Jed growled and her womb clenched as his tongue slicked over her bottom lip before pushing its ways inside again, taste testing her as he went along. The kiss went from hot to volcanic and one arm tightened around her waist and the other held the back of her head as if she might—crazy thought—have an inclination to go somewhere. There was no place she'd rather be but here in Jed's arms, under the control of his kiss.

She felt Jed's hand fiddling in her hair, felt him pulling at the band that held her hair up in its messy knot, and then her hair was loose, tumbling down her back. Jed wrapped it around his hand and tugged her head back, changing the angle of their kiss, taking it deeper and hotter and wetter. From somewhere far away she could smell her perfume in the air, mingling with his masculine cologne. Kissing him wasn't enough, she needed more. Pulling back, resentful because she had to momentarily stop kissing him, she yanked her dress over her head and then slammed her mouth back to his, sighing when her hard nipples pushed into his chest.

God, yes! More.

As if he was hearing her silent plea, Jed's hands skimmed over her flushed, bare skin and then they were at her waist, sliding under the band of her thong, pushing the scrap of fabric over her hips and down her thighs until gravity could take over and drop the panties to the floor. His hand explored her stomach, brushed over her landing strip and instead of going where she needed him to, he slid his hands over her buttocks and covered her cheeks, the tips of his fingers in lovely, indecent places.

Still kissing her, he bent his knees and boosted her up his body and her legs automatically encircled his hips as she gripped him with her thighs. And then she was naked and exposed, riding his still covered shaft. Moaning, she tried to push his pants down but Jed just shook his head, kissing her once and then twice before pulling his mouth away completely.

He looked down at her with eyes that looked feral; heavy-lidded and desperately determined. "Last chance to say no, honey."

McKenna wiggled her hips and choked back a scream as her feminine cluster of nerves stroked over his sex, sending lightning bolts through her system. "Not a chance in hell," she muttered.

Jed grinned. "I was hoping you'd say that." He brushed the hair away from her forehead in a curiously tender gesture before running his thumb over her full bottom lip, down the side of her neck, over her collarbone to rest on her distended, berry-pink nipple. “Then hold on ’cause we’re going on a helluva ride.”

“You promised to make me scream,” McKenna reminded him as he lowered her to the bed.

“I always keep my promises,” Jed told her, following her down.

He made her scream. More than once.

Chapter Nine

THE ONLY THING Jed really wanted to do the next morning was to stay in bed with McKenna, but he knew that he had carry on as normal, so he wrenched himself away from her perfect body shortly before seven, knowing that Daisy would soon be waking up. Going back to his room, he did his normal punishing routine of sit-ups and push-ups and after a quick shower, he headed downstairs. With a cup of coffee in hand, he walked around the house, looking for some evidence left behind by last night's intruder. As he scanned the grass, the flower beds, and the house, he thought about McKenna and the amazing night they'd shared. She was a giving and generous lover, demanding and submissive in turn and he'd never felt so sexually in tune with a woman before. He'd seemed to know, on a cellular level, how to touch her and she'd known exactly which one of his drive-him-crazy buttons to push. He wished, of course he did, that they could have more than one night but they couldn't; that wasn't the deal. Their one night was over far too quickly and he had to now act as her bodyguard, and not as her lover, because that was what was in her best interests.

His gut was churning and he couldn't discount the notion that there was something malevolent hovering in the air, waiting for the perfect time to strike.

Not finding anything that explained last night's noises, Jed stood on the back porch, sipping his coffee and smiling when he heard Daisy asking McKenna when he could take her swimming again. Jed didn't hear McKenna's reply but, judging by Daisy's loud groan, he presumed that she'd nixed that idea.

"Mattie!" Daisy cried and instead of walking back into the kitchen, he stayed where he was, happy to stand in the early morning sunshine and to let the cousins have some time together.

"Hey, McKenna," Mattie said. Jed frowned at her serious tone and wondered what was coming next. "You look different."

Jed wondered if McKenna was a kiss-and-tell type of girl and was relieved when she said: "New foundation, it's nice, isn't it?"

"Is it called Screwed? 'Cause I don't think I know that brand."

Jed winced at Mattie's sarcastic reply but McKenna didn't respond to her baiting. He slouched against the wall and stood still, unrepentantly eavesdropping. Over the years he'd acquired some pretty good information doing this.

"I think you should tell him to leave," Mattie stated. "He's building up this stalker thing so that he can play the big protector and so that you will sleep with him."

Really, was that what he was doing? Nice to know.

"Nonsense," McKenna replied after ordering Daisy to eat her eggs and not to play with them. "Jed doesn't play games like that; he calls it straight."

"He just wants to get into your pants," Mattie insisted.

Of course he did, he was a man and she was gorgeous.

"I'm just saying that you should be careful of him. You don't need him to stay on the premises; you're perfectly safe in your house at night."

"Jed doesn't think so.", McKenna countered.

"What does he know? He's just a photographer, Mac!"

"No, he's not," McKenna replied.

Jed frowned and waited for her to continue. What did she think that she knew about him?

"I mean, yes, he's photographer and an excellent one at that…we've all seen the proof. But he's more than that."

"What are you talking about?" Mattie demanded.

Jed told himself to relax; McKenna didn't know anything about anything. He could imagine her slim shoulders lifting and a tiny frown appearing between her eyebrows.

"Ignore me," McKenna told Mattie and his shoulders slumped.

"No, tell me! Drugs? Guns? Human trafficking?" Mattie demanded, her voice rising with excited horror.

I made a hell of an impression on you, didn't I?

"Don't be ridiculous," McKenna scoffed.

"Well, if you have your doubts about him then he definitely shouldn't be staying here! With you!"

"He's a bad boy, Cousin," Mattie added, her voice laced with concern.

McKenna didn't say anything for a long time. "I know, Matt."

"We talked about why you have to stay away from these types of men; I spent hours and hours with you working through why you are fatally attracted to men like him."

"He's not a bad man," McKenna protested. "He treats me well."

"And, like all the others, he'll still leave. You're just trying to recreate the past, McKenna. Your attraction for him has little to do with him and so much to do with you wanting to perpetuate the familiar."

Okay…whoa. What the hell was happening here? What was Mattie talking about and why wasn't Mac disagreeing with her? Jed waited for her to argue, to tell Mattie that she was wrong…but Mac remained silent.

When McKenna asked how the Miller dress was progressing, Jed had to hold back his growl of frustration. He wanted to know more, he wanted an explanation. And he'd painted himself into a corner because if he asked, then he'd have to admit that he was eavesdropping and that wasn't, well, cool.

And why did he care anyway? Mac was just good sex, someone he was giving a helping hand to. Mattie was right, he was leaving, he had work to do, *important* work. As soon as her stalking situation was resolved, he'd be gone. And if the idea of leaving didn't sound as appealing as it had when he first arrived in this town, then he'd damn well ignore it. He was getting soft, he decided; all the estrogen in this house was rubbing off on him.

Jed slipped down the steps, walked a couple of paces, and deliberately made a noise as he stomped up to the porch, giving the women ample warning of his arrival.

When he opened the kitchen door Daisy slammed into his legs and he swung her up to his shoulder, wincing when her delighted squeal shattered his ear drum. McKenna met his eyes, blushed slightly, and licked her lips. God, he had fond memories of those lips on his—*do not go there, moron!*

McKenna dropped her eyes, told Daisy to stop shrieking and him to put her down. Mattie, he noticed, didn't even bother to greet him. Instead, she picked up her cup of coffee and told McKenna that she was going to the salon to do some alterations.

Jed placed Daisy on the floor and handed his coffee cup to McKenna for a refill. "She doesn't like me much."

"She's just protective over me," McKenna defended her as he'd expected her to.

Jed pulled out a kitchen chair and dropped into it, lifting an eyebrow when Daisy immediately climbed up into his lap, straddled his knee, and continued to eat her breakfast. Daisy shouted a defiant "No!" when McKenna told her to climb down.

Thinking that it was easier to leave her where she was, she seemed perfectly at ease to just perch there. Jed shook his head at her, silently telling her to leave her as is. McKenna picked up her cup of coffee and sat down in the chair opposite him and, by the wary look in her eyes and the tremble in her fingers, he knew she'd realized that playtime was over.

"Were they worse than usual? The calls and emails?"

Jed nodded. "The calls were same old, same old. A voice

deliberately muffled and the messages he left were short, to the point. As per usual, nothing that could be directly tied to Daniels."

"And the emails?"

Jed leaned past Daisy and picked an apple from the fruit bowl and bit down into it. He crunched, took another bite and crunched again. "Long, tedious, repetitive. Vicious."

Jed lowered his apple and stared at her, his strong brows pulled together. "Now that's weird," he said, thinking aloud.

"What?" McKenna demanded.

"Why are his calls short and to the point and his emails vicious and long and…venomous?" Jed took three bites of his apple and placed his core on the side of Daisy's plate.

Seeing that Daisy was finished eating and that her hands were heading for his clean jeans, he took Daisy's sticky hands and wiped them with a paper napkin, mulling over the problem. Why the disconnect? Was it a time thing? Was he worried about his calls being traced that he kept them short? Why was this bugging Jed?

Daisy turned and lifted her chin up and waited. It took him a moment to realize that she was waiting for him to wipe her face so he quickly swiped the napkin over her mouth. Jed lifted her down to the floor still thinking that there was a strong disconnect between the calls and the emails.

"Go brush your teeth, Daze," he told her, tapping her bottom to urge her along.

Last night he'd thought that the emails were very personal…were they barking up the wrong tree here? He looked at

McKenna and frowned when he saw the gobsmacked look on her face as she watched Daisy leave the room.

"What?" he demanded.

God, had he done something wrong? Said something he shouldn't have? Was he presuming too much by telling her to brush her teeth? Jeez, he barely touched her. Was he being too familiar?

McKenna snapped her mouth shut and tipped her head to the side. "Are you sure you don't have any kids?" she asked.

What the hell…this again? "I'm pretty damn sure," Jed snapped. "Can we concentrate here?"

McKenna sent him another of her mysterious looks before nodding. "Okay, concentrating." She wrinkled her nose in a way that made him want to kiss the hell out of her. "What am I concentrating on?"

Jed pulled his head out of the clouds. "How personal did you get with Daniels? You said you went on a couple of dates…did you open up to him?"

McKenna frowned. "What do you mean?"

"Did you talk to him, like more than the normal surface stuff? Did you sleep with him?" He lifted his hands when McKenna's eyes cooled. "I'm not trying to be an asshole, Mac; I'm trying to find answers."

"No," McKenna replied, her voice curt.

Dammit, that was what he thought. "Are you in any doubt that Daniels is the one sending you the emails?"

"No. He keeps sending them from different email addresses but he always signs it the same way, uses that same phrase at the end."

I'm going to get you, bitch. Jed doubted that he'd ever forget it. Still, something was out of sync here; a puzzle piece was missing and he didn't like it. It couldn't hurt to dig a little more, to probe a little deeper. He'd rather do that than miss something crucial. "Tell me about any other significant relationships you've had."

"No way!" McKenna retorted.

He sighed, weary. "Mac, I'm not asking to bust your chops. Something is bugging me and I'm trying to work out what it is…just cooperate, okay? Just give me the highlights."

"There's not really much to tell." McKenna folded her arms and looked mutinous. When she lifted her face, he saw the fear in her eyes. "I really don't want to tell you, Jed. It's…humiliating."

"That's a pretty strong term, Mac," Jed said, keeping his tone mild.

"Don't tell me I didn't warn you. When I was nineteen, I had this boyfriend and we were crazy in love," McKenna said in a quiet voice. "He was horrible but I loved him. When I wasn't utterly miserable I was so happy."

Okay, that spurt of jealously was totally unreasonable. What the hell was wrong with him?

"He was diagnosed with Guillain-Barre; it's a rare disorder in which your body's immune system attacks your nerves. Anyway, he was so sick and he lost so much weight he could hardly walk and the drugs made him feel dreadful and *I was nineteen.*"

"You bailed," Jed stated, keeping his voice calm.

"Yes," McKenna said in a quiet whisper and he could hear the shame and the guilt in that one word. "I broke his heart and I broke his parents' hearts. They called me an unfeeling bitch with a heart as cold as ice but I couldn't…do it."

He leaned back so that the front legs of the kitchen chair lifted off the ground. "How long were you together?"

"Six months," McKenna admitted. She gnawed on her bottom lip before shoving her hands into her hair and speaking again. "I get it okay? I'm just like your father, useless in a crisis. I didn't stick either, Jed."

Shit. Jed blew air into his cheeks as he brought the chair down. She was nothing like his dad and he needed to convince her of that fact. "Mac, my father had been married to my mother for more than thirty years. He had two children with her. He'd made commitments, promises to her. In sickness and in health…baby, you were a teenager, faced with watching someone you loved in pain. That's a horrible experience and it would've taken an exceptionally strong woman to stick around. It has no comparisons with my parents and I can't judge you."

"I told him that I loved him," McKenna whispered.

"And you probably did, as much as a teenager could. Though I suspect that you were confusing sex with love." Jed smiled at her and was rewarded with a trembling, half smile back. "Could he be the one who has this massive hard-on for you?"

McKenna shook her head.

"You sure?"

"Yeah." She ran her hand over her face, her expression bleak. "He's had his revenge."

Jed frowned. "Explain."

"When he recovered, I begged him to take me back. He did. He treated me like crap and made my life miserable by constantly telling me that I failed him. When he had enough of me begging for the forgiveness he had no intention of ever giving me, he dumped me and moved in someone else."

Jed's fist clenched on the table. Five minutes alone with him, that was all he would need. "And Daisy's father?" he asked when the red mist cleared from his vision.

McKenna closed her eyes and he saw years of pain and regret drift across her face. *This would be worse*, and he steeled himself to hear the story.

"Another traumatic my-love-life-is-stranger-than-fiction story. Zoo was—"

Who named their child Zoo? "Seriously, that was his name?"

"Arthur Able Moya, son of Khaya and Jeanette. The Moya's started a little chain of fast-food stores called Afri-Aroma, heard of them?"

A rival to the golden arches, the Afri-Aroma fast-food brand was almost as big and occupied every corner the big M didn't. And McKenna had dated their son? Lofty company indeed.

"Go on," he urged.

"Everyone called him Zoo, mostly because he was like a caged animal. Spoiled, irresponsible, slightly crazy. He had the attention span of a gnat and he wasn't thrilled to hear he was going to be a daddy." McKenna tapped her nail against the rim of her cup. "When I got pregnant, I had to grow up and fast. I knew that Zoo was bad for me, would be very bad for my baby…he wasn't the most stable person around. I knew that I would have to be the responsible one, that I'd have to shield my child from his excesses. That meant I had to distance myself from him."

"Did you love him?" Jed quietly asked.

He had no right to know, didn't know why he was holding his breath waiting for her answer.

McKenna just shrugged. "Yes, no, I don't know. We had an intense attraction but was it love? Probably not."

"Where is he now?" Jed asked. "He's obviously not part of Daisy's life."

McKenna bit the side of her lip. "He asked me to abort her, told me that I had to choose him or the baby. The night I told him that I was going to ditch him and keep the baby, he left and went to the nearest club. According to our friends, he did at least ten tequila shots, had a couple of beers and did some coke. He left to go to another club and rocketed his sports car into a tree. The tree survived, he didn't."

Jed felt sick. "God, Mac."

McKenna placed her elbows on the table and rubbed her forehead with the tips of her fingers. "That's it. Two screwed up relationships with not very nice men." She rubbed harder, pushing her fingers up into her hairline. She looked up at him and tried to smile. "I'm fatally attracted to unavailable men. I love the challenge, the sense of adventure that walking on the wild side with them brings."

Was that what he was? A walk on the wild side?

McKenna rested the ball of her hand against her temple. "I'm easily bored and terribly curious. That's why I loved my time with Zoo, he was always up to doing something different, seeing a new place, trying a new experience. Though we were only together a few months, we skydived and learned to scuba, went kite surfing and tried different foods. Of course, Zoo also tried every drug available..." McKenna's words trailed off as she turned to look out the window. "Anyway, I lost the right to hop from job to job and town to town and experience to experience when I got pregnant with Daisy. Children need stability."

"Children need parents," Jed countered. "As long as they are with the people who love them they'll be fine."

"Mattie disagrees. She says that Daisy needs a base, a home, consistency. Rules."

Jed held back his snort. "And she's had how many kids? None? Kids need love, that's it. Trust me, I should know," he ended, his words bitter.

"Tell me about what happened with your dad," McKenna spoke quietly.

"You heard, the other night."

"Tell me the whole story," she quietly insisted. "Come on, I just bled over the table in front of you."

"A little quid pro quo, huh?" What would it hurt to tell her? It wasn't like it was a state secret or anything.

"The day that I found out my father had been having an affair? I was...crap...distraught is the best word I can find."

Jed surprised himself when the words flowed out of his mouth with no hesitation. For the first time in, well, ever, he didn't censor his words and it felt strange and liberating. "My mother died desperate for my father's attention and my father was screwing a woman younger than me. Admittedly, I'd never particularly liked my father but I always respected him. He walked the talk, you know? He had strong values and he lived them…or so I thought. That day, I felt like the world had spun off its axis."

Jed couldn't believe he was telling her this; he wanted to stop talking but the words just kept on coming. "I flew back to the UK and went straight to my girlfriend's place; we were pretty serious, we'd been involved for a couple of years and I thought that I'd, eventually, end up with her."

She just looked at him, her eyes wide, surprised and, he was glad to see, without a smidgeon of pity within them.

"I was, obviously upset. I wasn't crying but—" Okay, he'd been close to tears but he was damned if he was going to admit that. "—I was gutted. She didn't bother to ask what the problem was, she just told me to buck up and to get a grip. I was in the Special Air Service, a spec ops soldier and I wasn't allowed to fall apart. That she was the girl in this relationship and I didn't get to be hysterical."

McKenna dropped her hands back to the table and moved one hand so that it lay next to his, slender and pale alongside his broad hand. He watched, fascinated, as her pinky finger hooked his. It was a tiny touch, an infinitesimal link but it grounded him, gave him strength. Somehow she knew that words were superfluous and absolutely not what he needed from her.

They were quiet for a long time before McKenna spoke again. "She never asked you what happened?"

Jed shook his head. "Nope."

McKenna bit her lip and tipped her head to the side. "Can I say something?"

Could he stop her? He didn't think so. He shrugged. "Sure."

"That *bitch.* God, I would've *slapped* her." The words burst from her and her eyes flashed with fury. "Please tell me that you booted her off the nearest cliff."

Jed, touched at her immediate defense of him, almost smiled. "I walked out. The next day, while she was at work, I cleared my stuff out of the apartment and broke up with her when she came home from work. Then she turned on the waterworks and apologized and…wah, wah, wah."

McKenna disconnected their fingers and leaned back in the chair. "Thank you for telling me that, for letting me know that I'm not the only emotional screw up in the room." Her teasing, affectionate smile took the sting out of her words.

"Yeah, well…it's not something that I talk about often." Or ever. That was the first time that anyone had heard his sob story and she, definitely, would also be the last.

"Do you talk to anyone? At all? About anything? Your work—your photography work and the other stuff you do—who are your friends, the people you talk to?"

Jed had to think for a moment, wondering how to answer her. He had friends from the SAS he was still in contact with but they shared little more than war stories. He had agents within Pytheon that he frequently worked with, but he wasn't friends with them. So who did he talk to? Seth mostly.

"I'm pretty self-contained," he told McKenna.

"No, you're not. You're paranoid and secretive and incredibly emotionally distant."

Jed flicked her a quick look, now feeling awkward. Where was this conversation going? "I'm not sure what you want me to say," Jed said, rubbing the back of his neck.

A sad smile touched McKenna's lips. "Well, you didn't deny my accusations."

"Nothing to deny," Jed admitted. "I am all of the above and more."

McKenna rested her chin in her hand. "Why?"

Jed's entire body tensed. Okay, this was more than enough. "Can we talk about something else?" he demanded, pushing away from the table and abruptly standing up. He walked over to the kitchen door, leaning his shoulder into the doorframe.

"Looking for a quick exit?" Jed, frowned, not sure to what she was referring. McKenna smiled. "You immediately walked toward the door, suggesting that you are ready to bolt."

Jed looked from her to the door and realized that he had subconsciously, done exactly that. Well, shit. "Look, McKenna, I'm not a talk-ey, share-ey kind of guy. This was a once in a lifetime thing, don't expect it to happen again."

He looked for the right words, feeling uncomfortable

and exposed. "Talking…emoting… doesn't accomplish much and I'm in the business of results." How did he explain this and if he did, would she understand? The image of Jax's battered, discarded body half in and half out of that grimy bath in Islamabad flashed onto the big screen of his mind. It took every ounce of control he had not to shudder. "I've see some bad stuff, and that's putting it mildly. When you've walked through that hell you tend to slot things into perspective, very quickly. If it's not life or death or arterial blood spray, it's just not that important. Talking isn't important. Getting the job done is."

"But talking is important to those who love you," McKenna pointed out. "Leah needs you to talk to her, to be her big brother…she is, well she isn't bleeding but she is hurting. About your mom, about your absence. You can't dismiss her pain because it isn't life or death or arterial spray."

Jed felt the impact of her words, somewhere within his soul. He wished he could shrug off her observation but he couldn't. Seeing the world in black and white made life easier for him but he forgot that for civilians, there were a million shades of gray.

"She's also worried because you are so solitary, Jed, so damn alone."

"I like it like that," Jed replied, stubbornly. Yeah, okay, living here in her house, with a stroppy, independent funny kid—living "normal"—wasn't as hard, as foreign or as strange as he'd thought it would be.

But he knew himself well enough to realize that this

wasn't a life he could do full time; he'd go stir crazy if he couldn't get out into the world, into the dusty villages and the steaming jungles, looking for that elusive photograph, that one image that told a thousand stories. He'd be lost without that surge of adrenalin, without the chase, his camera always primed and ready.

And he'd miss the work he did for Pytheon. Maybe not as much as he would the photography, but he enjoyed the work, the mental skill it took to recover the object he'd been sent to find. He liked restoring…well, order. But if he was forced to choose between the two he'd choose the photography; he would gather up his false passports, his stashes of cash, his arsenal of weapons in the various places he'd stashed them around the world and he'd walk away from Pytheon before he gave up his camera.

Holy crap. That was unexpected. He'd honestly thought that it would be the other way around; that he'd ditch the photography and sink further into that clandestine world. What had changed? And why?

How much of this had to do with McKenna and these unfamiliar thoughts and emotions she'd stirred up by just breathing? Ten, twenty, eighty…a *hundred* percent? He simply didn't know.

McKenna stood up, walked over to him, and clasped the back of his neck with one hand. Standing on her tiptoes, she arched her neck so that her mouth was next to his ear. "You don't have to be alone, Jed. Like everything else, it's a choice and if you want to talk, then I promise I'll listen."

It was tempting, it really was, he thought as his arms

snaked around her waist and he pulled her so that she was flush against him. But nothing good ever came of talking. He knew this; he had the scars to prove it.

Chapter Ten

OVER THE NEXT few days, Jed couldn't settle. He felt like his skin was too tight for his body and his senses were jacked. Colors seemed brighter and odors were sharper and his gut was humming. It was the same sensation he had before he snatched a person or an objective, before he fired his weapon, wrapped an arm around a neck to render someone unconscious. He was super aware, super buzzed, a walking, talking radar, constantly scanning his environment for trouble. The phones calls, the text messages, and the emails had stopped and that made him very, very nervous. No one with that much rage just stopped for no reason. It was too much to hope, and too dangerous to assume, that McKenna's stalker had been hit by a bus and that the harassment was over. Because trouble, he knew this like he knew how to handle a weapon, was just around the corner. His sixth sense, gut instinct, guardian angel—whatever the hell that insistent voice was that spoke from the depths of his soul—was screaming that he stay vigilant. As a result, he was in a constant state of readiness which was, frankly, exhausting.

Remaining alert and focused was also intensely difficult when you had a little girl who wanted to play and a lot bigger girl that he wanted to play very adult games with. He wasn't stupid, he saw the lust-filled looks she sent him, he knew that he just had to slip inside her room and into bed with her and she would welcome him with open arms. He couldn't understand it but she seemed to want him as much as he wanted her…

Staying away from her was torture. But he couldn't afford to be distracted, not when her and Daisy's lives were on the line. He'd rather die before seeing either of them hurt. That was not a dramatic statement but just an absolute truth. Because he couldn't imagine a world, couldn't live in a world, that didn't have them in it. It was that simple. He'd bleed out before he allowed anything to happen to them.

And Jesus, it didn't help that there seemed to be movement on the situation in Pakistan. One of his trusted, but super paranoid sources had reached out to him, using a text messaging app he'd installed on his mobile. Despite the end-to-end encryption both over the air and in the actual phone, all Mohamed stated was that it was a good time for Jed to return to Islamabad.

Reading between the lines, Jed knew that Mo had decent information and a solid lead. He wouldn't risk his time, and pissing him off, for anything less.

He should move out but he couldn't leave McKenna. His life would mean shit if something happened to her. Jax's revenge would, simply, have to wait.

He'd get to it, and hopefully get some solid information on The Recruiter, but only when he knew that McKenna, and Daisy, were safe.

They'd, somehow, become his highest priority. How the hell had that happened?

IT WAS JUST past nine and McKenna walked into her renovated salon and saw Jed staring out the picture window. McKenna looked at his bleak face and wondered what he was thinking about. He looked so sad but so determined and she wished that he would talk to her. Opening her laptop, she powered it up, thinking that she wanted to know him; she wanted to know what made him scared and what made him vulnerable, what made him happy. She'd thought, just once or twice, that she and Daisy did. She'd noticed that when the three of them were together, in those quiet moments at the end of the day, or in the kitchen in the early morning, the tension left his body and that a small smile played peek-a-boo with his mouth. His eyes looked almost tender and she could easily imagine them being a family.

But that was an impossible dream because while she loved Jed—God, she didn't know how that happened but it had—she couldn't live with a man who had so many secrets, whose heart and mind was a firmly closed book. She needed openness and communication and affection and Jed had been alone for so long and emotional self-sufficiency was a habit for him. And not one that he intended to break for them.

She couldn't live like that, always wanting more. She wanted the midnight talks and the tears, the honesty of being vulnerable. She didn't want to live with Superman; she wanted to live with a man, the good, the bad, and the ugly. She could cope with them being apart, she knew that Jed would never be a nine-to-five type of guy but when he was with her, she needed him to be *with* her.

She loved him. She so wished she didn't.

She had to start letting him go, she had to teach Daisy to do the same. How did you tell a little girl that Jed could stay in her heart but not in her life? That this man she adored wouldn't be, in the long run, good for her mommy's emotional well-being, her mommy's heart? She couldn't tell her that and she wouldn't…but she could continue to remind Daisy that he was leaving, that he wasn't a permanent fixture.

Jed turned and half smiled at her as she walked across the room to her desk. She was beginning to know his expressions and instead of seeing the usual desire for her in his eyes, he looked a little unsure and a lot troubled; like he had far too much on his mind.

"Mattie will be joining me in a little while; we need to discuss a new design," McKenna said, looking at her sketchpad that sat next to her laptop.

Jed nodded. "I'll work in the kitchen; I have some photos to edit."

He stared at her for a long time and McKenna wondered what was on his mind. Because it was obvious that something was…

"The other day I heard you talking to Mattie and you were talking about me. She said something about you trying to recreate the past, that your attraction to me is you just wanting to perpetuate the familiar…what did she mean?"

Whoa…talk about an out-of-the-blue comment. McKenna took a moment for his words to sink in and make sense and when they did she swore under her breath. Dammit, that conversation had been four days ago and Mattie had been talking out her hat. "What she said doesn't apply to you, Jed."

"What did she mean?" Jed demanded, jamming his hands into the pockets of his shorts, his gaze direct and unrelenting.

She wasn't going to get away without an explanation, she realized.

Dammit.

McKenna sat down on her couch and crossed her legs. "I've mentioned my father to you once or twice, but what I didn't tell you was that he was very rebellious, a lot wild, and a huge rebel. I idolized him, adored him with a ferocity that bordered on obsessive. But I might have exaggerated our level of closeness. For a long time, in my eyes, my dad could do no wrong. I adored him through the broken promises—and there were many—and I watched him treat a series of girlfriends pretty badly. I felt lost when he died and…"

She didn't want to tell him, not this. Mostly because she just knew that, unless she bared her soul, he'd misunderstand.

"And?" Jed prompted.

He wasn't going to let her off the hook, dammit. "Mattie helped me realize that I choose men with similar traits to my father. She also thinks that I choose unavailable men because my father was, essentially, mostly unavailable to me and also because I want to, subconsciously 'redo' the relationship I had with him."

Jed turned his back to her and looked out of the window. "And do you think that she's right?"

"I think she *was* right. I did do that. With you, I think it's different—"

"Mac," Jed interrupted her but the tone of his voice had her head snapping up.

Either he didn't want to hear how she felt about him or something else had grabbed his attention. Judging by the fact that his eyes didn't leave the street, she was choosing option B. She wasn't sure if she felt relieved or sad or a combination of both.

McKenna noticed that Jed was standing to the side of the window and she realized nobody from the street could see him observing the road. "What car does Daniels drive?"

McKenna thought for a moment. "A black Benz but sometimes he uses his fiancée's Prius."

"Sky blue?" Jed rattled off the car tags and McKenna nodded.

She'd seen that car pass her house many, many times and she could recite the tags in her sleep. "Is he outside?"

"It's his second drive by," Jed replied. "He's looking for a parking spot."

McKenna's heart thumped off her rib cage. "He does that sometimes. He finds a parking place and just sits there, looking at my house. Creepy as hell."

Jed stepped back and looked at her. McKenna swallowed at the determined look on his face and thought that here was the real Jed, finally. Hard and tough, resolute and determined. Despite his cargo shorts, and black-and-white button down shirt worn over a white tee, he looked every inch of the spec ops warrior he was.

"Want to bring this to a head?" he quietly asked.

McKenna wanted to say no because she knew that when her stalker situation was over, Jed would be leaving her life. She hadn't had nearly enough time with him; she'd only slept with him once. She wanted more drugging kisses, hard hands, incredible orgasms. She wanted more…she wanted a lifetime.

But she couldn't prolong a dangerous situation because she wanted more time with Jed. That was irresponsible and reprehensible but she was tempted. Damn she was tempted.

"Mac?" Jed spoke again. "You want to see if we can resolve this?"

McKenna nodded, licking he lips. "Yes. How?"

Jed rocked on his heels. "I'm going to leave, out the front door, as if I'm in a hurry to be somewhere. I'm going to walk to the end of the block, duck out of sight, and make my way back to you using the backyards."

"It's daylight, you'll be seen, and the Hartwells have dogs," McKenna pointed out.

Jed's look told her that he'd been in a lot stickier situations and to trust him. Funny how they'd started communicating without words. But damn, she still liked it, loved it, when he opened up, when he revealed the softer, more vulnerable man beneath the alpha male, hardass exterior. Damn that stupid woman who'd told him that emotion was unattractive. She'd like to slap her senseless.

"Mac!" Jed's sharp voice brought her back to the here and now and she mentally shook herself. Right, stalker, outside. Plan of action.

"I'm listening," McKenna told him. "You're leaving and going to come back in via the back door."

"He'll wait a couple of minutes and then he'll approach the door. Give me at least five minutes to get back to you, then if he rings the door, invite him in and let's see what he does."

McKenna put her hand to her throat. "God, Jed…I—"

Jed walked over to her and placed his hands on her shoulders. "I'm not going to let anything happen to you, I promise."

McKenna looked up into his gold eyes. "If something happens to you, it might get ugly."

"Nothing is going to happen to me," Jed told her with a reassuring smile. "Let's worry about you, okay? I'll be here for you, I promise. But keep your head, think the situation through. Do not panic. I'll come through the back door and the video camera on my phone will be rolling, so try to get him to incriminate himself."

"This is like TV," McKenna whispered.

Jed dropped a kiss on her temple. "Yeah, the most boring episode in history. You'll talk to him, I'll cover you, and if he puts a finger on you, I'll beat him into a coma." Jed quickly kissed her lips. "Don't overthink this; just give me five minutes before you open the door, okay?"

McKenna felt her stomach sink to her toes as Jed walked toward the door. She wasn't happy about this and she had a very bad feeling that this situation was about to go up in flames. She wasn't a spec ops soldier; he couldn't throw a plan at her and expect her to get with the program.

She needed to think, to plan… "Jed, wait!"

Over his very strong shoulder Jed sent her a confident wink. "Trust me, Mac. I'm not going to let you down."

CRAIG DANIELS STOOD in her hallway, his hands in his pockets and a scowl on his face. With the front door open behind him and his pouty expression, McKenna suddenly realized that she wasn't scared. Of him or this situation. Jed had her back, she knew that, but even if Jed wasn't here, she knew that she still wouldn't be scared. Why not?

"What do you want, Craig?" she asked.

"I want to know why you accused me of stalking you. Do you know what that's done to my reputation? My relationship with Haley?"

"You shouldn't have sent me threatening emails or left countless phone and text messages then!" McKenna replied, her voice hot.

Craig pushed a hand through his dirty blond, floppy hair. "Look, I'll admit that in the beginning, I was a bit intense and I sent you a couple of emails but I didn't leave any phone messages or threaten you even once!" Craig closed his eyes and when he opened them again McKenna was shocked to see that they were a bit watery. God, was he on the verge of tears?

"My job is important to me, McKenna, and my colleagues are looking at me as if I skin bunnies for breakfast. Haley has postponed our wedding again. I'll admit to a couple of silly emails but *I've never threatened you once!*"

He's convincing, I almost believe him. "But—" McKenna frowned when Mattie stepped through from the kitchen.

She gave Craig a long look before turning her gaze to McKenna. Now that was an expression she'd never seen on Mattie's face before. Hard, cold, distant.

"Where's Jed?" Mattie asked.

McKenna started to tell Mattie that Jed would be back in a minute—*she knew that like she knew her own name*—but bit back the words. Daniels sounded convincing but he could still be snowing her. Maybe Mattie could help her to get him to confess.

"Leah called, said that she was having second thoughts about the wedding. So Jed ran over there to talk convince her to call it off," she lied.

Mattie's frown cleared. "So he's really not here?" she clarified.

Jeez, how many times did McKenna have to say it? And what was with Mattie's strange smile? She looked weird…

"Jed is not here," she reiterated. McKenna turned back to Craig and lifted her shoulders. "Look, I'd like to believe you but…"

"I'm not your stalker!" Craig cried, his voice shrill in the hallway. "How can I make you believe that?"

"Maybe this will help," Mattie said.

McKenna looked at Mattie and struggled to make sense of this crazy picture. Why did Mattie have a gun and why was she pointing it in her direction? This was her cousin, her best friend… she shouldn't be pointing it at her, it could go off.

"I couldn't have planned this better," Mattie said, her tone and eyes and face, Arctic-cold.

As it finally dawned on McKenna that Mattie was threatening her, pointing a gun at her, Jed, silent but deadly, rugby-tackled her to the floor. Mattie shrieked, Craig screamed, and McKenna watched as the pistol skidded across the floor to disappear under the hall table. Mattie screamed louder when Jed placed his knee in her back, his weight easily keeping her pinned to the floor.

McKenna, unaware that tears were rolling down her face stared at her cousin, her best friend. Mattie? Mattie had been behind the threats. "It was you? But you love Daisy, you love *me*."

Mattie turned her head and McKenna stepped back at the hatred in her eyes, the sneer on her face. "I love Daisy and I hate you. You shouldn't be her mommy; you're not a fit parent."

"What the hell? Where is this coming from?" McKenna yelled. "I'd die for Daisy! You know how much I love her. Why would you do this?"

"When you started dating again I knew that you would choose badly, you always do. You wouldn't recognize a good man if he had the words tattooed on his forehead! And you proved it when you picked up that nut job!" Mattie sneered in Craig's direction.

"Pot, kettle, black," Jed murmured.

"Daisy is growing up and I couldn't run the risk of having her witness, being exposed to your crazy relationships. I couldn't risk you putting her in harm's way. Eventually you'd form a relationship with someone—someone bad—and I'd be pushed away and he'd have control over my Daisy."

"She's mine!" McKenna shouted. "*My child, always and forever! Mine! Not yours.*"

"She would've been mine, if you died."

The rocketing pain and the crazy confusion wanted to drag her under but McKenna forced herself to think. "Because I named you as Daisy's guardian in my will. The will I made around the same time I dated Craig," she said as the pieces of this macabre puzzle started to drop into place.

"With you gone I'd be Daisy's mother," Mattie pouted. "I had it all planned, a stalker had terrorized you for months with emails and phone calls. He broke into your house and destroyed the dresses and the salon—"

God, this was crazy! "You did that? Why? You made those gowns."

Mattie shrugged. "I hired someone and I would do *anything* for Daisy."

Up to and including murder. McKenna put her hand on the wall to steady herself, unable to drop her gaze from this stranger inhabiting her cousin's body.

Mattie's expression changed and she looked hurt and upset. "You lied to me, you said Jed was out."

"I was trying to get Craig to confess…" God, why was she trying to explain? This woman had tried to kill her so that she could raise her daughter. McKenna felt the bile rise and thought that she was going to be sick.

"Hang in there, honey," Jed told her. Turning to Craig, he barked out another order. "Daniels! Unplug the cord from the telephone and then use your cell to call the cops."

McKenna was vaguely aware that Craig was obeying Jed's orders but she felt like her legs were turning to rubber, that the air was getting thinner. But she kept her eyes on Jed's face and his gaze kept flicking between her and the cord he was winding around Mattie's wrists.

"Ten seconds, babe, I'll be there now. Hang in there, okay?"

From a place far, far away McKenna watched Jed stand up and their eye contact was all that was keeping her grounded, from shattering into a million shards from betrayal. Mattie had a gun; she'd been intending to kill her. Craig too, probably. She swayed and then she felt Jed's hands sliding around her waist and she slumped against him. She placed her face into his neck, too shocked for tears, too hurt to speak.

She'd lost her best friend, her cousin, the last connection to her father, to the Dixon family. McKenna's arms tightened around Jed's neck. And, when this horror stated to recede, she'd lose Jed, too.

This time she didn't think she could stand it.

LATER THAT DAY, McKenna lay curled up in her bed, shivering too much for sleep. It was barely eight but she was exhausted and completely and utterly spent. After the police arrived and hauled Mattie off, she'd spent the rest of the day at the police station, answering a million questions from what seemed like a million detectives. Separated from Jed, she felt lost and alone and so very, very cold. The day had consisted of just long blocks of waiting interspersed with the same questions posed in a hundred different ways.

It was late afternoon before they'd taken her back to her house in a police car and she'd immediately left to fetch Daisy from the friend who'd collected her from playgroup. Feeding and bathing Daisy had kept the shakes at bay and had allowed her to switch off for a little while but after she'd put Daisy to bed, she'd climbed into the shower. But the steaming hot water hadn't managed to warm her core and she'd stayed there, sitting on the floor and sobbing, until the water ran cold.

Mattie had been a constant and comforting presence in her life for the past four years, her cousin but also her best friend. Sure, Mattie had been dogmatic and cautious and very conservative but she'd genuinely believed that she had her, and Daisy's, best interests at heart. Mattie's pragmatism and…and…*solidity* had been a great counter foil to her impetuous nature. Four years and she'd never once suspected that Mattie saw herself as anything other than her best friend and Daisy's beloved cousin/aunt.

But, obviously, her cousin was—what was that expression that Jed used?—bat shit insane. She'd seen it in Mattie's crazy eyes; she'd heard it in the phrases she'd screamed when the police took her away. The mask had cracked and the monster underneath had been exposed.

McKenna whimpered. If Mattie's plan had succeeded…if Jed hadn't been there. Another bout of shivers racked her…Mattie would've become Daisy's guardian…

Oh God…

She needed Jed, she thought, lying in bed, tears rolling, her stomach clenching against the waves of nausea. She wanted to fall asleep on his shoulder and sleep for a hundred years. And after a century had passed, she wanted to wake up in Jed's arms and spend the rest of her life loving him. Was that too much to ask? She wanted Jed, she needed him.

As if she'd verbally called to him, Jed appeared in her doorway, dressed in nothing more than a pair of sweat pants. Saying nothing, he walked over to the bed and pushed the pants over his hips, stepping out of them as he pulled back the covers and slid in. She immediately moved closer to him, sighing as his warm body immediately started to dissolve the cold, hard, terrified core inside her.

"Baby," Jed whispered, hauling her up so that she lay flush against him, his arms around her, his mouth on that point where her jaw and neck met. "You okay?"

McKenna shook her head. "No," she replied. "I feel sick and sad and a part of me is still scared."

"Normal," Jed murmured, his hand pushing under her thin pajama bottoms to palm her butt in his hand.

"Stay with me tonight," McKenna asked him, her lips against his. "Make love to me, distract me, take this all away."

She saw him swallow, felt him rise against her. His strong arms lifted her so that she lay on top of him. "I can do that."

This, McKenna decided as his mouth moved against hers, as his tongue slipped inside, *this is what I want, what I need.* His mouth on hers, his hands separating her butt cheeks so that he could touch her intimately, confidently, in the right place with the right pressure. He could take her from feeling sad to feeling excited, from hurt to turned on. He was what she'd always been looking for, the one man who would never bore her. McKenna sucked in her breath as he pulled her thin tank top over her head so that he could put his mouth to her nipple. She'd never completely know him, she realized, he had depths that would keep her intrigued for a lifetime. She didn't need her freedom, she needed him.

Jed was what she'd been searching for, she thought as he pushed the strip of her thong aside to pull her down onto him, stretching her as he filled the empty places in her soul. He was her fantasy, her reality, the one relationship that wouldn't make her feel confined.

He filled her, McKenna sighed, physically and mentally. Emotionally. He moved her, in every way that mattered. McKenna opened her eyes as she sat up to straddle him and looked down into his. He reached up and tucked a long curl behind her ear. She knew that her feelings were written all over her face and couldn't help it. She loved him. She wanted forever with him.

Jed sat up and his action pushed him further inside her and she gasped with pleasure. He gripped her hips and rested his forehead on her collarbone, hiding his face from her. He groaned as she moved and she thought about asking him to stay, about asking him to love her. She was about to speak when his hand moved between them and he touched her clit and she bucked and writhed, her concentration entirely focused on the pleasure that hovered a hair's breadth out of reach. He allowed her to tip over before flipping her over and started to the build her up again.

He made love to her until she was too exhausted to talk and that was, as McKenna realized before she drifted off to sleep, probably the point.

Chapter Eleven

JED LEFT MCKENNA to sleep and, after pulling on some shorts, his sneakers, and a T-shirt, slipped out of the house to indulge in a long run. It was hard to leave the house and he had to remind himself that she was safe, that the threat toward her had been neutralized. His heart lurched, unable to stop the memory of seeing that Berretta pointed in McKenna's direction. The look on Mattie's face had told him that she'd been very prepared to use it; he'd seen that same cold, calculating look before. Thinking that he was out of the picture and no threat to her, she'd been prepared to commit a double murder. As she'd later admitted, she'd intended to stage the scene so that it looked like a murder-suicide and she might have gotten away with it.

Jed picked up his pace to try and outrun the shiver that danced up and down his spine. He hadn't really warmed to Mattie but he'd never, not once, thought she was the source of danger, and on more than one occasion he'd left McKenna and Daisy with her ...fuck! Anything could've happened and he felt sick to his stomach. Nothing happened, he reminded himself. They were both safe and he'd done his job. Jed stumbled to a halt and placed his hands on his knees. Except that she wasn't a job, she—and Daisy—

were...

Not.

A.

Job.

He didn't know what she was but, judging from the look on her face last night, he knew that she fancied herself in love with him. Maybe he fancied himself in love with her. But there was too much emotion swirling around them to think clearly. The last couple of weeks had been a time of heightened stress and the hectic chemistry they experienced just ramped up the passion. He was her protection and that stroked his ego and she was grateful for the protection and that made her feel mushy. And, as they'd been discussing before he spotted Daniels out the window, there was the whole reliving her relationship with her father issue.

He felt like he was being pelted with a million emotions, about to collapse under the weight of what he was feeling. And that was the point, he had to stop emoting and start *thinking*...

Even if they threw caution to the wind and tried to make a—*you can say it, moron, it won't, actually, hur*t—relationship work, he knew that it couldn't last, it wouldn't last. He needed to travel, needed to continue his work with the magazine; he wouldn't be able to stay in one place, month after month, year after year. McKenna had a business in Simons Town and a daughter who needed to be in one place. Give them a couple of weeks, months, and the bloom would fade from the rose. He couldn't give them what they needed; someone who was always around, someone who was there day in and day out. Daisy deserved a full-time dad and he would just drop in and out of their lives on an ad hoc basis.

And McKenna needed a man who would talk to her, be with her, open himself up to her. Who shared every part of his life with her. God, he'd yet to tell her what he actually did for Pytheon…

She needed someone who could take the pressure off her when being a mom became too much, someone to share that stress and the joy. He couldn't do that when he was halfway across the world. She also needed to dig and pry and immerse herself in a relationship; she loved with all of her heart and she wouldn't be satisfied with a part-time, uncommunicative ex-soldier, full-time thief. She needed someone who was affectionate, spontaneous, open…fun. A part of him desperately wanted to try and be that man but whenever he tried to imagine it, he felt like his air supply was being cut off. It would mean sacrificing his freedom, giving up some control.

If there was ever a woman who could tempt him into doing just that, it was McKenna but, judging by the fact that his stomach went into free fall at the idea and that his throat closed, he didn't think he could do it. He'd known her for about a month, he couldn't make life changing decisions after just spending so little time with her. That was…crazy. Irrational. Emotional.

Jed felt his phone vibrate and pulled it from the case attached to his bicep. Swiping the screen, his heart lurched when he saw the brief message from Mo.

BB returning to the city within the next week. Suggest

you return.

Shit. Jed stared up at the sky, reading between the two lines of Mohamed's brief message. For some reason, God knew what, Barker was planning to return to Islamabad. Instead of tracking him to dusty, craphole villages, through countryside that was treacherous and unforgiving, he would be able to find Barker, with Mo's extensive network of informants, with minimal effort. He just needed to get his ass on a plane.

As for McKenna? And Daisy? nip this in the bud, this was cleanest way to do it. And Mo's message meant that he had to leave now, today...while he still had the strength to do it.

It was better this way. It really was. And, maybe one day he'd believe his own lies.

SHE WASN'T GOING to cry, McKenna told herself, deeply aware of the tears that were threatening to spill. She had to be strong for the little girl in her arms, the one whose face was buried in her neck, her thumb in her mouth. Jed walked down the stairs, his pack over one shoulder, his face serious and his eyes bleak.

He has to go, it was the nature of the beast. McKenna knew this but it didn't make it any easier. She wiped her eyes with the back of her wrist and prayed that he wouldn't try to touch her, that he wouldn't try to hold her. She couldn't bear that. If she touched him, she would fall apart and she couldn't afford to do that. She had Daisy to look after, a life to lead, a business to sort out. Her life didn't stop because her best friend tried to kill her.

"Are you going to be okay?" Jed asked her, dropping his rucksack to the floor.

No, but she wasn't going to tell him that. "I'm fine."

She knew that he didn't believe her.

"I need to go but in a week or two, I could come back if you need me to."

"Now you're just being kind." McKenna chewed the side of her lip. "This isn't something that I'm going to be able to sort through in a couple of days, Jed, or even a week or two," McKenna stated, as calmly as she could. "This is going to hurt for a long time and you can't heal me."

"But I could be here for you."

"For how long?" McKenna cried. "Until the next shoot, the next recovery job?"

He'd explained, very briefly what he did for Python—Pantheon?—something about finding objects, people and information that were lost. It was what he didn't say that told her the most: it was dangerous, risky and sometimes illegal. She wasn't an idiot, she knew that there were dangerous jobs out there and it took smart but dangerous men to do them, and she'd never thought that Jed was a Boy Scout. He'd told her that he'd crossed some lines but he tried to stay on the side of the angels as much as he possibly could. He'd expected her to be horrified, to be ashamed of him but he didn't realize that she knew who he was, knew the essence of him. Yes, he was hard and tough and determined and could be an enemy nobody in their sane mind wanted to have. But he was also kind, and funny, and protective and loving…

"I have to do this, Mac. I need to."

She knew that, she did, she saw the shadows in his eyes, she knew that Jed had a dragon or two to slay.

McKenna shoved her free hand through her hair. "I'm sorry, I know that I'm not as important as your missions but I need you too. I need you to hold me at night, to come home to me, to listen to me. You are my heart and I'll always need you, in one way or another."

"Jesus, Mac, I don't know what to say. I don't know if I can give you what you want and more importantly, what you and Daisy need. But I can come back, maybe we can figure it out." She felt her heart splintering and it took a huge effort for her to shake her head. "No. That's not going to work for me."

It was one of the few times that she'd caught him off guard and if she wasn't so sad, she'd find it a little funny. Jed rattled; it was a rare and beautiful thing.

"I don't understand."

"A relationship would never work between us, with only one of us needing the other. I need you to need me; I need you to talk to me, for me to be your soft place to fall. I can't be the one taking everything, I have to give, too."

Jed stared at her and his eyes cooled. McKenna placed Daisy on her feet and told her to go into the kitchen, that she and Jed needed to talk. Daisy looked from Jed to her and eventually turned away to do as she was told, her shoulders slumping as she walked away.

"You're asking me to give you everything," Jed said, his voice raspy with emotion.

"Since I'm offering our hearts, it's the least you can do!" McKenna cried. "I love you, Daisy loves you, all we're asking is for you to love us back. To trust us, to be your family."

Jed rubbed his hands over his face. "You're asking too much, Mac."

"No, Jed, I'm really not." McKenna sighed, intensely weary. "But I can't force you so…" She walked over to the door and opened it, gesturing for him to walk on through. "I think it's time you left."

Jed closed his eyes, his expression pure agony. He glanced toward the kitchen. "Daisy, I need to…say good-bye."

"Make it quick," McKenna ordered, "and don't make her any promises that you can't keep."

McKenna wrapped her arms around her waist as Jed walked into the kitchen. She heard his low voice, heard Daisy's quiet sobs and at that moment she hated him; hated him for making them love him, hated him for leaving, hated him for breaking their hearts and leaving them alone. She'd never forgive him for leaving her, them.

And she'd never love anyone like she did him. Nobody would ever be able to love him like they did.

Oh, God, this hurt. On top of Mattie's betrayal, this was like pouring acid into a gaping, bone deep wound. But she would cope, McKenna thought, straightening her shoulders as she heard his approaching footsteps. She was McKenna

Dixon and she'd coped with everything else life had thrown at her.

After all, this wasn't her first ride in the my-life-sucks rodeo.

Jed picked up his backpack and pulled the strap over one broad shoulder. She would not fling herself into his arms and beg him to stay. She had more pride than that, besides, he didn't love her and he didn't want to stay. He'd proven that by taking the first new assignment that Pytheon offered him.

She was very low down of his list of priorities. "Thanks for saving my life," McKenna said as he approached her.

"Least I could do," Jed told her, picking up his hand to cup her face. "Take care of yourself, okay?"

"You too, Slick."

McKenna wondered if that was indecision she saw in Jed's eyes but she suspected that it was just her active imagination working overtime. Jed didn't respond but bent to kiss her temple, resting his head against hers.

"Take care, Mac," he whispered into her hair. "Call me if you need anything. Ever."

I need *you.* McKenna caught the words just before they left her mouth and swallowed them. "Same goes, Jed."

But she knew that he would never ask. Because Jed didn't need anything from anybody.

THE INFORMATION HIS trusted source Mohamed had turned out to be a steaming pile of shit. Barker had never had any intention of returning to Islamabad and if Jed's head hadn't been up his ass, he would've realized that. Why return to a city where the police wanted your head on a platter for the brutal and attention grabbing murder of a beautiful blond Westerner? Barker was young but he wasn't a fool.

After a week in Islamabad chasing his ass—missing McKenna, missing Daisy and as miserable as hell—Seth, knowing he was going nuts, handed him another assignment, one that had nothing to do with Barker. So, to do his job, Jed was in Peshawar, northern Pakistan and one of the most dangerous cities on earth and he was weaving his way through the afternoon shoppers. He was waiting to meet a guide who'd agreed to accompany him into the Federally Administered Tribal Areas or, in shorthand, FATA. His cover was that he had an assignment to photograph the Buddhist archaeological sites Takht Bhai and Pushkalavati to swing through the Khyber Pass and then on to Darra Adam Khel, hoping to get decent shots of the famous gun makers of that city.

The real reason why he was in this part of the world was because Seth wanted him to put eyes on Faisel Mustafa, the third son of a Saudi billionaire who was now living and working as a gun dealer in Darra. His father wanted him to return home and Pytheon had been asked to get someone to deliver that message. Jed was the delivery boy. It wasn't a particularly dangerous assignment, he'd had worse in the region, but nothing in this area of Pakistan was ever a walk in the park.

But he'd taken it because he had to keep moving, had to

keep busy because if he didn't, he'd slowly go mad. It had been three months and three continents since he'd seen McKenna and Daisy and the memories of them weren't fading. Every day he missed them more and was constantly bombarded by thoughts of what they were doing...had Daisy learned to swim yet, how was McKenna coping with the fact that her oldest friend had wanted her dead, was she dating someone else...*was another man sleeping in her bed?*

The thought slammed into Jed and he came to an abrupt halt, his fist resting in his solar plexus. *I can't afford to lose my concentration*, he berated himself, *not in one of the most dangerous cities on earth.* It was a stupid, foolish thing to do and one way to find himself in more trouble than he could handle. It could find him dead.

What the hell was he doing here? He looked around. His was the lone white face and he was automatically regarded with suspicion and more than ten men had hissed threats at him already this afternoon. He was in a strange city in a strange land and this wasn't where he wanted to be.

Face the truth. Admit it. Where he wanted to be was halfway across the world, with McKenna. And Daisy. Being a lover and if he was really, really lucky, a full time husband and father.

"Mr. Jed?"

Jed whipped around and looked into the smiling, but calculating face of the middle aged man standing in front of him. Like every other Muslim in the city, he wore salwar kameez, the traditional loose fitting robe and pants eminently suitable for the climate. Jed tipped his head to the side, waiting a beat before responding to his enquiry. There was something about this man's eyes that had him hesitating, a cockiness in his demeanour that raised goose bumps on his arms.

The man thumped his chest. "Tahir. You Jed Hami-on?"

Close enough. Jed looked around, not sure why he was hesitating about this man, this ride. A friend of a friend of Mohamed, his source back in Islamabad made these arrangements for him so why was he suspicious? And he was just a photographer working for a well-known and international magazine, he was paying in good, old USD so what was his problem?

Right time, right place, the guy had the right name. For all of that Jed was super reluctant to get into his battered, held together by a prayer and duct tape car. *You're either getting paranoid or old but you either have to walk away or cop to being Jed Hami-on.*

"Yeah, I'm Jed."

A flash of satisfaction hit Tahir's eyes and Jed knew that if he got into the car, he would be walking into a situation he might not be able to control. Needing time to think, he dropped to his haunches and pretended to retie the laces of his shoes. He had no doubt that Tahir or, more likely, whoever was paying Tahir had no intention of driving him into the FATA, if he made it out of Peshawar he'd be damn lucky. So, the question remained, was he being targeted for being an American citizen, a well know photographer who could be ransomed for a hefty pile of cash? Or, God forbid, did someone know that he was more than the outward person he presented himself to be?

Did anyone in this country know his connection to Pytheon, know that he was hunting Barker? Mohamed, his chief contact and go to person, thought of him as his well-heeled, slightly naïve photojournalist friend and frequently chided him on the risks he took to get a story, to find justice for Miss Jax. She was gone, her boyfriend was lost, he should let it go, Mohamed pleaded. Jed was pretty good at reading faces and he was 90 percent sure that Mohamed was on the side of the angels, if the Islam religion had angels.

But there was always that 10 percent. And the kidnap-for-ransom scenario.

Jed tied his other lace before straightening. He didn't have any weapons on him except for a knife strapped to his ankle and his hands and feet. If he was overpowered he'd be in deep, deep, bad shit.

"Are you okay, Mr Jed?"

Jed saw the hand coming toward him, noticed the middle three fingers were missing, the bent pinky finger. A scar that ran down the inside of his index finger, raised and angry looking. Jed saw white thighs being pulled apart, that mangled hand pushing down on Jax's naked flesh as he rammed into her, heard her piercing scream, her pleas for mercy.

Jesus. Tahir was one of the men who raped Jax, he was part of the cell Bo Barker joined. That meant that he was no longer the hunter, Jed was now the hunted. How the fuck did they know about him? And how much? Did they think he was a journalist looking for a story or did they know he was an Pytheon operative? Either way, he'd finally, finally made contact with Barker's cell and he was damned if he was going to lose it.

Jed stood up slowly, immediately going into battle mode. Keeping the expression on his face as pleasant as he could, he slid his hands into the pockets of his pants and his right hand curled around his phone, holding down the volume button for ten seconds. In twenty seconds or so, an SOS signal would be sent to the nearest cell tower and in another ten all the bells and whistles in the Pytheon control room would light up like the Fourth of July. There weren't any Pytheon operatives in the area that he knew of but Stone, the big boss, had enough contacts in the area to scramble some support for him. That support might be CIA, Delta Force or the marines or even the Pakistani police. He didn't care who came running, as long as they carried shit that went boom.

"You ready to go now, Mr Hami-on?"

"Yep." Jed reached for the handle of the back door and wasn't surprised to find the door locked. Tahir would want him in the front, where he could be controlled. Tahir held out his hand for Jed's backpack and Jed forced himself to hand it over. It contained his favorite camera and some long range lenses that he'd hate to lose but nothing that couldn't be replace. He always, always kept his wallet and passport on his person.

Besides, everything he valued most was back in Simons Town. His partner and lover. His daughter.

Jed looked Tahir in the eye as the man opened the passenger door. He smiled slowly, as he ambled to the car. Fuck this and the boat it came in on. He was ending this, today.

And then he was going home. Where he was damn well going to stay.

Chapter Twelve

IN SIMONS TOWN, McKenna stood at her stove, idly stirring scrambled eggs. It was a stunning day with the sky so blue she just wanted to stroke it. Later it would be hot but for now, the early morning temperature was perfectly pleasant.

The sun was shining, the birds were singing and, because she'd found an amazingly talented seamstress, she had someone to sew Leah's dress. It took all she had to fulfil her obligation to Jed's sister. Since that day Mattie tried to kill her in order to take her child, McKenna couldn't draw, couldn't meet with happy brides, couldn't look at a wedding dress without feeling faint. And nauseous. And so damn scared.

She didn't have a business or a lover but she had her child. Thank God. Daisy was fine, she was fine, life was freakin' fine…

What a load of rubbish.

McKenna turned the gas off and all but flung the pan away. She was miserable, Daisy was miserable…Jed's absence had left a massive gaping hole in what was her and her baby daughter's life.

They missed, him, they needed him but he was off playing happy photographer or super spy or something else somewhere dangerous. God, if she could she'd kick him. How dare he drop into their lives, make them fall in love with him and disappear? What was with that shit?

"Asshole," McKenna muttered, shoving her hand into her hair and fighting the tears burning in her eyes.

"Mommy?"

McKenna release a long, silent curse before turning, pulling a smile onto her face. Daisy stood in the doorway to the kitchen, her big blue eyes radiating distress.

McKenna's anger evaporated instantly and she shot across the kitchen to pick up Daisy, touching her forehead and cheek to check whether she had a temperature, to do a mommy-scan. "Are you okay, sweetie? Are you hurt?"

Daisy shook her head. "Not me. Jed."

McKenna frowned, not sure what she'd heard. "Say again, Daze?"

Daisy pushed her face into McKenna's neck. "Jed has an owie."

McKenna's heart stopped for a moment, recognizing the truth in that statement before her rational brain kicked in. "Honey, Jed isn't here so you can't know that."

"Can too." Daisy shook her head so violently that her curls bounced. "Jed hurt, Mommy. I want Jed to come home."

Me too, honey, me too. McKenna rubbed Daisy's back. "Jed is fine, honey. And, baby, we talked about this. Jed's job is far away from here, he can't just drop by. This isn't his home, baby girl."

"Is too."

She agreed. The only person not with the program was Jed himself. Daisy pulled away and her eyes slammed into McKenna's, reflecting a stubborn fierceness she prayed she'd never lose. They looked at each other for a long time and then Daisy's expression cleared. Smiling, Daisy placed both her hands on McKenna's cheeks and smiled, suddenly pure sunshine. "Jed's okay now. And he will come home, Mommy. Just be patient, 'kay?"

How the hell was she supposed to respond to that? There was nothing she could say. If she tried explaining that Jed wasn't coming back, then she'd have to deal with Daisy's howling sobs—she didn't think she could go through that again—and if she agreed with Daisy then she'd be giving her false hope. It was better to remain quiet and hope that Jed gradually faded from Daisy's memory until he was a distant, sweet memory.

She wished that would happen to her but she knew she wouldn't be that lucky. Jed would forever be imprinted on her heart. Missing him, mourning him was something she now did, something she was.

TAHIR PULLED A weapon on him as soon as they got settled in the car, which pissed Jed off but wasn't unexpected. He could've liberated him of the weapon in two seconds flat but then he'd lose the opportunity of finding Barker so Jed just leaned back in his seat and waited for the movie to play out.

The situation got complicated when Tahir pulled over and another man jumped into the backseat, leaned between the front seats and jammed a revolver into his rib cage. New guy was young, the weapon was old but, judging by the distinctive smell of gun oil, had recently been cleaned. It would do the job.

They'd counted five people in that room with Jax Petersen, he bet that he was now keeping company with two. One against two wasn't bad odds, provided he could put something between himself and the ends of weapons that went bang.

Jed felt the world speed up and slow down, both at exactly the same time. His hearing sharpened and Jed understood the occasional word of the rapid fire Pashto between his two kidnappers. He was super aware of his surroundings, noting landmarks. If they relieved him of his phone, which they would, and he managed to escape he had to know where he was. Heading east past a massive stadium, crossing what looked to be a substantial highway. Southeast now…

A market and a, God, was that a burger and pizza place? He'd kill for a decent slice…

The gun jabbed into his rib and Jed winced. Maybe using the word 'kill' in any sentence could be postponed until he was out of this jam. Tahir swung the car into a side street, practically putting the car on two wheels and gunning it down a crowded street, woman and children scattering. God, he was a shit driver but if he crashed the car, it wouldn't be a bad thing since their weapons would be out of play.

But, in this maze of pastel-poo colored houses, he'd never be able to find Barker on his own. And no one would dare help a foreigner, a blond foreigner, in these parts. That was like signing a death warrant. Jed looked down, saw the brown finger on the trigger of the gun against his side and wished these clowns would shut the hell up. One false move and that finger could jerk against the trigger and he was history. His biggest regret would be not telling Mac how much he loved her, that walking away from her and Daze was flat out stupid.

Blah, blah, New York, Blah…wait what? Jed frowned, concentrating on the words flying around the car. He'd definitely heard the word New York. Yep, that was an America, and Python? Jed tensed, his concentration absolute. Inshallah—God willing—Islamabad, New York again. Yep…Python. Jed didn't think that they were talking about snakes in America.

Pytheon. These asswipes knew who he worked for. And what, exactly, did that mean?

Before he could think this latest development through, Tahir stood on the brakes, whipped the car into a mini driveway in front of a flat roofed house and Jed shot forward, instinctively placing his hand on the cracked dashboard to keep balance himself. In the space of three seconds he saw the twitch of a drape in the window directly ahead of him, a flash of pale European skin, that the house was set back from the road and relatively secluded and that both his assailants were distracted. Lifting his arm, he slammed his elbow into the face of assailant number two and whipped around in his seat, his fist connecting with Tahir's throat. Tahir's eyes widened, his eyes flashed with panic and he lifted his hands to his neck, to trail his fingers over his crushed windpipe.

Knowing that Tahir would spend the next minutes sucking air down a pipe that was now the size of straw, Jed turned his attention to the threat behind him. The gun was lying between the two seats and Jed grabbed it, briefly thinking that blood looked good streaming from the bastard's nose. Tears rolled out of his eyes, over his mouth and into his now bloody beard. But broken nose or not, he was still a threat. As were the tangos in the house behind him.

As long as he lived, Jed never knew why he chose to go low at that precise moment but was forever thankful that he did because the bullet meant for his head slammed into Backseat's head, creating a perfect hole in the center of his forehead. Damn good shot, Jed acknowledged. He was just glad his head wasn't in the way as it passed through the windshield.

Jed glanced up, saw the now blue face and slumped body of Tahir. The man was hovering on the edge of consciousness and there was nothing anyone could do for him, not now. But he could, and would, save himself.

Jed dropped his hand and patted the floor beneath Tahir's feet for the semi-automated Glock Tahir pulled on him earlier. The rest of this demonic crew would be on their way and he needed more fire power than the old revolver. He was, crappit, a bit of a sitting duck. Jed's hand curled around the barrel of the Glock and he let out a quick sigh of relief. No more than twenty seconds had passed since they pulled up—funny how time dragged out when you weren't having fun—and he'd soon have company. He had to know what he was up against so Jed snapped off the rear-view mirror—his wrist made a lot smaller target than his head—and bullets flew over his head and the rest of the windshield disintegrated around him. Yep, lifting his head was a very bad idea.

Tilting the mirror, Jed watched as three tangos—one with very white skin and blue eyes—stepped out of the house, AK 47's raised to their shoulders. Shit. That wasn't good. He was, dammit, stuck where he was.

He needed a distraction, something big that would take their attention off him for, God, half a minute. That was all he needed. There were gas canisters next to the house and if this were a movie, he'd shoot one, the house would go boom and he'd walk away looking hot. But, alas, a bullet wouldn't pierce the canister's armor. Why weren't they shooting, why hadn't they riddled the car with bullets? What the hell were they waiting for? The only reason he could think of was that they wanted him alive, to send a message. To who? Since he didn't have a family *anyone knew about*—Mac and Daze were two new additions to his life—and since he heard his company's name earlier, he could only think that someone wanted to send Pytheon a damn big up yours by discharging his ass.

He could take out one, maybe two but there was no way that he could take out a third.

Shit, *Mac, I love you…*

He heard the blast of a bullet, and in the small mirror saw the bullet connect with a chest and a tango drop to his knees. Tango two dropped two seconds later and training and instinct took over and he bolted up, aiming at Barker. He fired and the Glock responded with a reassuring jerk. Even more satisfying was seeing Barker spin around, falling to the ground, kicking up dust.

Jed exited the vehicle, saw that the third tango was down and looked around. Fuck, who was on his side and why? Not that he was complaining. Staying behind the thin barrier of the car door, he scanned his surroundings. The shots came from his right, roof height but the roof was empty.

The sniper, because that was what he was, had to have been here before he arrived, had to have known about Barker, about the cell. Dammit, what the hell had he stumbled into? Jed pulled his eyes back to Barker, his bright blond hair glinting in the sunlight. In the quiet morning, he could hear his low groan, his whimpered prayers. Judging by the gaping hole in his chest, Barker would be meeting with his god in a few minutes.

Jed jerked when he caught a flash from a muzzle from the corner of his eye and watched as a bullet plowed into the back of Barker's head. Barker, it seemed, would be a few minutes earlier for his appointment with death than he'd estimated.

"Now, would be a good time to leave, Mr Hamilton."

The voice was Western, calm, distant but held a command that Jed couldn't ignore. He still couldn't see his guardian angel but he wasn't going to argue. He'd had a free pass and sure-as-shit he was going to take it.

Reaching back, Jed whipped Tahir's turban from his

head and wrapped it around his own—his blond hair was a friggin beacon in this city. Pulling himself into a low crouch, he ran back to the rickety fence, bailed over and whipped around the house to his left. He'd avoid the road for a while and prayed that if the locals saw a turbaned man wearing Western clothes running through their yard, they'd leave him alone.

They did and five houses later, Jed, now dressed in a salwar kameez he'd swiped off a washing line and pulled it over his T-shirt and jeans, wasn't as conspicuous as he was ten minutes before.

Jed saw a group of men making their way to a mosque and hurried to catch up to the group, staying far enough from them not to draw their attention but close enough so that people might think he was one of them. The crowds thickened as they neared the mosque so Jed pulled away and stood in the doorway to a shop, closed for prayers. He dug his phone out of his pants pocket.

His call to Seth connected immediately.

"Well, you're still alive." Seth's calm drawl settled his heartbeat and pulled a wry smile to his face.

"Just. Thanks to someone who was already in position," Jed briskly stated.

Seth's lack of an instant response was telling. "Come again?"

"I'll make this quick." He needed to get the hell out of Peshawar, henceforth to be known as the seventh level of hell. "I arrived by car, disabled the two tangos in the car. One of the tangos in the car has a mangled hand, you can see it on the video of Jax's murder. I was pinned down in the car and three tangos exited the house, including Barker."

"You saw him?"

"Sure as shit. My guardian angel took out two tangos, I shot Barker but didn't kill him. Before I could think what to do, my GA takes out Barker with a head shot and suggested that I remove myself from the scene. Which I did. I heard sirens in the distance, I presume they were for me?"

"Yeah. I managed to scramble a SEAL team to help you but they are still at least twenty minutes away."

"The sniper knew my name so who do you think he belongs to?" Jed asked.

Jed could imagine Seth's powerful shoulder's lifting and falling. "Someone with kick ass connections, that's for sure. He could be part of any group, an alphabet agency or a black ops mission, or someone on contract. I'll get Stone to work on finding out who and why. I don't like not knowing who we are in debt to. Did you see him?"

Jed snorted his disbelief. "The dude was a ghost and it all happened within five minutes." Jed gripped the bridge of his nose. "You've got another problem, Seth."

"And that would be?" Seth's voice was low and soft but as deadly as hell.

"The tangos knew that I was Pytheon, knew exactly who I was. While I was hunting them, they were hunting me. I think they wanted to take me alive to send you, and Stone, a message.

"And that begs the question, why would a terrorist cell want to grab the attention of a powerful international security company? What's the link?" Jed continued.

"The Recruiter." Seth said the name like a curse word.

"Bingo. This dude is playing games, Seth, nasty, dangerous games."

Seth swore. "I hear you. I don't know what to do about it, yet, but I hear you." Seth was silent for a beat or two and then his voice returned to normal. "Come home and we'll figure out the next step."

Except that New York wasn't home. It hadn't been for a long time, possibly not ever. Home was McKenna and Daisy, living with them, loving them. Home was where they were. Jed stared down at the dusty pavement, at the frayed hem of his jeans peeking out from underneath his tunic. To be with Mac meant that he'd have to compromise. He couldn't have his cake and eat it, too. Something would have to give and he knew that giving them up was not an option. Ever.

For the first time in weeks, months, Jed smiled. "I'm not coming home and I'm not coming back to Pytheon. I'm done."

Seth swore. "Reason?"

"I'm going back to Simons Town, back to McKenna. Hopefully, I'll manage to talk her into a happily ever after."

"And this from the man who categorically stated, not that long ago, that he'd rather face a firing squad than get married," Seth replied, his voice amused. "I can't say I'm surprised, no one can do this job forever and I knew that you were nearing your expiry date. When I heard you talk about McKenna I knew that you were a goner."

And he was happy to be gone.

"I'll call you when I get somewhere less conspicuous and we can work out my exit plan." Jed looked around. "I have no idea where I am so I wouldn't mind some help getting out of this shitty city."

"Head west toward the market, and look for the burger place on the corner. I've arranged for a local to pick you up and take you to the airport. I'll have tickets waiting for you."

"They'd better bloody well be for Simons Town," Jed muttered, annoyed to see his hand trembling, that he felt hot and then cold. And damned tired. His adrenalin high was winding down. "I'm going home, Seth."

"I know, bud. Trust me, I'll get you back to your girl as soon as I can."

Girls, Jed silently corrected him as he started to walk. His girls were waiting for him. Seriously, he could not wait.

SIX FIFTY-SIX, SIX fifty-seven…McKenna watched the digital numbers of her bedside clock tick down and she slapped her hand on top of the device as the alarm shrieked. She'd been awake for most of last night and now, when it was time to get the day started, she wanted to sleep. She needed just another hour…The house was quiet which meant Daisy was still asleep, thank God. McKenna quickly reset her alarm and immediately fell into a light doze, dreaming of Jed.

But dreaming of Jed hurt as much as missing Jed and after forty-five minutes, she forced her eyes open and sat up, pushing her hair out of her face and wiping tears away with the tips of her fingers. Dammit. She hadn't slept well for nearly a hundred days and she was sick of Jed interrupting her days as well as her nights...

God, she still missed him; three months and counting and, unlike Daisy, the longing for Jed just got worse rather than better, she thought as she climbed out of bed. Memories kept ambushing her, the smell of his skin, that little smile of his, the way he'd held her up against that wall and kissed the hell out of her. *Don't think about it,* McKenna told herself, *just go downstairs, have a cup of coffee and get on with your life.*

One of these days you'll stop missing him, she thought as she walked into the kitchen. Hopefully one day soon. *You'll stop imagining him sitting at your kitchen table, smiling at Daisy...*

As she was about to pour coffee into her cup, the realization that she hadn't heard Daisy rising—that Daisy hadn't woken her up with her customary morning snuggle—struck her. Yet her daughter was wide awake, hair brushed, dressed, and eating eggs and bacon made for her by...Jed.

Jed. Real Jed, not imaginary Jed.

McKenna turned around slowly and there he was, as large as life and twice as sexy, sitting at her kitchen table. The coffee cup slipped through her fingers and shattered as it hit the floor, spraying coffee over her bare feet and the hems of her cotton pants. She could feel the heat of the coffee on her skin but she couldn't think beyond the fact that...

Jed. Was. Back.

"Don't move," Jed commanded in his caramel over steel voice.

He pushed his way to his feet and McKenna just stared at him, her eyes flying over his face, over his body. He'd had a haircut, she noticed, and his jaw was covered with a three- or four-day beard. He was wearing old jeans and a plain red T-shirt and she thought she could lick him up with a spoon.

"Mama, Jed camed home. I told ya," Daisy shouted. Daisy patted her rib cage. "He has an owie here."

Jed's eyes widened. "How the hell does she know that?"

McKenna shook her head. "I have no damn idea."

Daisy eased her way off her chair, heading to McKenna.

"Stay where you are, short stuff," Jed told her, picking her up and placing her back on her chair. "I don't want either of you cutting your feet."

"'Kay," Daisy happily agreed, shoving another mouthful of egg into her mouth.

Jed reached McKenna, placed both his hands on her waist, and with a quick movement lifted her up and into his body. She gasped and her eyes crossed as he held her against him, his eyes staring down into her. Soft eyes, vulnerable eyes…

"Hi," she said, tongue-tied and more than a little overcome with emotion.

The corners of his mouth tipped up and her heart tripped in response. "Hi back. How are you?"

"Good." McKenna made herself place her hands on his chest and tried to put some distance between them. "You can let me go now."

Jed shook his head and placed one arm under her butt and lifted her so that her eyes were level with his. "God, you feel good." He held her easily with one arm while he touched her cheek with the fingers of his other hand.

McKenna's arms looped around his neck and she rested her forehead against his. "Jed, I can't think. You need to put me down…this is all a bit much. Why are you here?"

Jed walked backward with her and whirled around and placed her on the center island, pushing her legs open, and moving to stand between them. He placed his hands on either side of her hips and leaned in close, keeping their eye contact. "We have so much to talk about," he said, his voice low and slow, "but, I swear, if I don't kiss you I'm gonna flatline."

Unable to resist the desperate desire in his eyes, McKenna tipped her face up and sighed when his mouth, finally, finally covered hers, his lips on hers, his tongue sliding against hers. She felt his hand in her hair, holding her head in place, the fingers on her hip digging into her skin. After a hot, far too-brief kiss, Jed lifted his head and sent her a rueful grin. "I'd like nothing better than to take you, right here and right now, take it deeper and hotter but there's a little girl in the room who is watching us with wide eyes."

McKenna looked over his shoulder to see that Daisy was indeed watching them with undisguised interest. She pulled a face at Jed when Jed banded his arm around her waist, easily lifted her and deposited her on a chair next to Daisy.

Daisy tipped her head back and pursed her lips at Jed. "Kissy, Jed," she demanded.

Jed grinned in delight and dropped a quick kiss on her pursed lips. Daisy beamed and McKenna's heart rolled over. Picking up Jed's cup of black coffee, she took a big sip and watched as Jed, quickly and efficiently cleaned up the mess on the floor before pouring her a fresh cup of coffee.

He sat down opposite Daisy and handed McKenna her coffee. "So, you'd be interested to know that I've met the woman I'm going to marry," he said, conversationally.

McKenna tried to swallow her smile of sheer delight, tried to ignore the building excitement and bubbling heat in her stomach. He was going there? *Already?*

"That's nice." She knew that she couldn't hide the excitement in her eyes. "You just kissed *me*. How would she feel about that?" she teased.

Jed's smile was tender. "I think she'd be okay with it. She's also funny and gorgeous and sexy and I can't imagine being with anyone but her. I can't imagine loving another woman as much as I love her. She makes my life; she *is* my life."

Mac closed her eyes at the emotion in his voice, hearing the tremble, the vulnerability that underscored his words. "Mac, look at me."

McKenna felt the tears in her eyes and blinked them away, concentrating on the love she saw on his face.

Jed brushed a tear off her cheek with his thumb, his face sober and serious. "So, will you marry me?"

McKenna nodded frantically, whispered a hurried yes, and burst into tears as she fell into his arms.

After Jed had mopped up her face, he explained to Daisy

that McKenna's tears were happy tears and that he was going to be around for the rest of their lives which resulted in Daisy bursting into tears herself. Jed, calmly and capably mopped up her face as well and after giving her another hug, sent Daisy to the backyard to play.

"You're going to be a good dad," McKenna said, her voice wobbly. Realizing the importance of that statement, she bit her lip as he resumed his seat at the table. "You do realize that we come as a package deal, that you're going to become an instant daddy as well as a husband?"

Jed sent her one of his slow, slow smiles that flipped her stomach over. "Yes, I think I've realized that."

McKenna wrinkled her nose at his gentle sarcasm. "And you're okay with that?"

Jed stretched out his long legs and linked his hands behind his head. "Do I look like I have a problem with it? I can handle Daisy, and any other kids we have, Mac."

Yeah, he could, McKenna realized. He could handle anything. Sure he was a bad boy, she didn't think that he would ever lose that edge but, better than that, he was a good *man*. He was her rock, her protector, her warrior and soon to be—whoo-boy!—husband. The desire in his eyes told her that what he'd most like to handle right then was her but as much as she'd like to sneak upstairs and reacquaint herself with his wonderful body, they couldn't. They had some talking to do but after she—they—dropped Daisy off at preschool they could come back and spend the rest of the morning in bed.

But, crap, she had an appointment at ten…well, before

and after her appointment, then.

Jed's laugh was infectious. "I really like the way you think, darling."

Oh, he was far too cocky, even if he was newly engaged and looking relaxed and so happy. *I did that,* McKenna thought, properly happy herself. But she couldn't resist teasing him, just a little. "I was thinking that I have an appointment at ten."

"You were working out how much time we had before and after and I'm going to use up every minute," Jed told her, as arrogant as ever.

Well, when he was right he was right, McKenna admitted.

Jed stood up, walked over to the kitchen door to check on Daisy, who was lying on her back in the grass, talking to her favorite doll. "Does she miss Mattie?" he asked, his voice sober.

"Yes. Horribly. She's also missed you."

He looked at her, emotion blazing from his face. Love and frustration and more guilt than she liked to see. "And you? Do you miss her?"

"Mattie?" McKenna bit her lip and nodded her head. "I do. She's in a psychiatric hospital being evaluated to see if she's fit to stand trial. Apparently all she talks about is Daisy." McKenna pushed her hair off her forehead and sighed. "It's been horrible; lonely, tough. My best friend, my cousin, tried to kill me and I lost the man I loved shortly afterward. It was…hard. Horrible."

Jed walked back toward her and crouched on his

haunches in front of her. He rested his forehead on her knee. "I'm sorry; I'm sorry I left you. I'm sorry I put my career in front of your needs…I was…. scared."

McKenna pushed her fingers into his hair. "Of what? Being loved?"

"Yes." Jed looked up at her. "Because you mean more to me than anyone ever has, you have the power to hurt me as no one ever has before. You know me Mac, you've seen me weak, you've seen me scared—" Jed saw that she was about to protest but shook his head. "When I saw Mattie pointing that gun at you, I aged about a hundred years."

"But you saved me." McKenna frowned. "I don't want to talk about her and that day…I want to talk about you and us and our future."

Jed stood up, lifted her from the chair, sat down, and pulled her down so that she was straddling his thighs. "Talking about our future, I've resigned from Pytheon; I won't be taking assignments from them anymore." He squeezed her thighs with his big hands and kept his eyes on her face. "I'd like to keep taking assignments from the magazine but if you can't live with me being away then I'll do something else."

McKenna felt her jaw drop. She searched for words to make an adequate, sensible reply but nothing except one word came to mind. "Why?" she whispered.

Jed didn't hesitate; he just looked at her and simply said, "Because you, and Daisy, are my home. Because I love you. Because I've realized that life means little without you and short stuff in it. That I'd rather go through hell with you than be in heaven and away from you."

"Oh, Jed." McKenna placed her hand on her jaw. "How often will you be away? And for how long?"

Jed shrugged. "It depends. Some are quick assignments, some can be up to two or three or four months away."

McKenna remained silent, quickly running scenarios in her head. Then she jumped, knowing that he would catch her. "Want some company?"

Jed frowned, confused. "Sorry? What?"

"Could Daisy and I come with you when you're away for months?" McKenna asked.

Jed looked astonished and equally delighted. "You'd do that, for me? But what about school for Daisy and your business?"

"My appointment was with another designer who is going to make me an offer to take my stock off my hands. Leah's dress is done—"

Jed's eyebrows shot up. "You actually got her to sign off on a design?"

"Yeah but she hates it. I know she does but she won't admit it. Like you, your sister is stubborn." Seeing that Jed was about to argue that point, she waved her words away. "Anyway, I'm shutting down my business; I can't look at a wedding gown without wanting to vomit."

Jed ran a comforting hand over her hair. "Oh, baby."

"I'm going to need to do something, sometime in the future, but right now I just want to do something new, be somewhere else…with you. Daisy is years away from needing any formal schooling and what she needs now I can do."

McKenna played with the buttons on his linen shirt. "I think that what I need, what we need most, is to be together."

Jed reached up to place a hot, sexy, open-mouthed kiss on her lips. "I agree and if you change your mind, then we go to Plan B. And if that doesn't work, then there are still twenty-four letters to hitch a plan to after that." He smiled and kissed her again. "I'm a soldier and we're nothing if not adaptable." He glanced at the big clock on the wall behind her and sighed. "Daisy time."

He brushed her hair off her cheek and smiled. "Since you're going to be giving up your business, is there any chance of you canceling your appointment and us spending the morning in bed?"

McKenna grinned at him. "Yeah, that I can do. As long as you promise to make me scream again."

"Scream and sigh and moan and..." He rested his forehead on her collarbone and groaned. "God, how long does it take to get Daze off to preschool?"

McKenna picked up his wrist and squinted at his watch. "Fifteen minutes if you hurry."

Jed lifted her up and off his lap and stood up. "I'll do it in ten," he promised on a quick grin, grabbing Daisy's satchel from off the table.

"Hey, short stuff, let's go. And if you hurry I'll take you swimming later."

McKenna heard Daisy's squeal of laughter as Jed swung her up and onto his shoulder, jogging across the patch of grass to the side gate of the property. Gorgeous, masculine, *hers.*

Oh, yeah, she so could watch him for the next year or two.

Or sixty.

Epilogue

THREE MONTHS LATER, McKenna walked into the luxurious hotel suite and kicked off her shoes, grateful to sink her weary feet into the heavy pile of the carpet. Jed shrugged out of his tuxedo jacket, loosened his tie but McKenna could see that he was a long way from feeling relaxed.

She was the only one who realized that Jed, despite his smiles and the obvious attention he'd given Leah in his role of "man of honor," still had some major reservations about Leah and her marriage. Well, it was done, and it had been a spectacular wedding, so different from their private wedding on a beach in Thailand three months ago with only Daisy in attendance.

"Leah looked absolutely fabulous." McKenna said, walking toward Jed and sliding her arms around his waist. "Suggesting that she wear your mom's gorgeous wedding gown was a very clever idea, darling."

"I have them occasionally," Jed said, dropping a kiss onto her head.

His hands linked behind her back as he held her so that they were up close and personal. They spent a lot of time being up close and personal, she thought smiling into his dress shirt. It was her favorite place to be.

"Daisy looked like she had fun," Jed said.

"Mmm," McKenna said. "It was nice of Zoo's mom to fetch her from the reception and for her to spend the night with them. They've invited us for brunch tomorrow morning, by the way."

Since their retirement from their business a few months before, Zoo's parents had returned to Simons Town on a permanent basis and had thrown themselves into retirement and that seemed to include being doting grandparents. McKenna was happy to let Daisy spend as much time as she could with them since she knew they they'd soon be leaving for the Australian Outback and she wouldn't see them for a while.

Thinking back on the evening, McKenna sighed. It had been a fairy tale wedding, complete with tuxedos and ball gowns, fantastic food, great music, and witty speeches. The bride had looked like a Disney princess and the groom like Prince Charming but something seemed off. She couldn't put her finger on it but, like Chicken Little, she'd spent the entire evening looking over her shoulder feeling like the sky was about to fall down.

Jed's big hand cradled her jaw and lifted her face up. "You okay?" he asked, his eyes soft and tender.

She wasn't going to tell him what she was thinking; besides it was probably just his unease rubbing off on her. "Just thinking about the ceremony and the reception. It was all so beautiful."

Jed frowned. "Are you regretting the fact that we got married barefoot on the beach? If you want to, we can do the church and white dress thing."

McKenna shook her head, her heart gooey with the love she felt for her bad boy. "I had the most wonderful wedding in the world and I wouldn't change a thing." She stood on her tiptoes to brush her lips against his mouth. She pulled back before he could take the kiss deeper, her fingers on his jaw. "You've got to let her go now, Jed. She's married, you had him checked out by Pytheon and they didn't find anything..."

Jed's eyes narrowed and his expression turned stubborn. "I'm still not convinced that he's all that he says he is."

They'd discussed this a hundred times before but she'd do it a hundred more if it made him feel more at ease with Leah's marriage. "Darling, the general used his sources as well to check him out and there's *nothing* there."

"My gut is still screaming."

McKenna hid her wince. She trusted his gut implicitly. "There's still nothing you can do. She's married; you have to let her go." McKenna placed her hands on his shoulders and jumped, wrapping her legs around his waist. Jed caught her, held her and she saw his eyes liquefy and deepen.

"Enough of the beautiful bride in her fabulous gown, I'd like your attention on me, Mr. Hamilton."

"That's never a problem, my delightful wife." Jed's hand slipped under her scarlet cocktail dress to toy with the thin cord of her thong before slipping down between her butt cheeks to rest on that hot, throbbing bundle of nerves.

"Yeah, that's exactly where I like your attention," McKenna said, dropping an open-mouthed kiss on his lips. She pulled back and looked at him, love and gratitude in her eyes. "Love you so much; I love being yours. I love our life."

"Me too, you make me so damn happy—dammit," Jed muttered as McKenna's eyes widened.

Holding her with one hand, he pulled his cell phone from the pocket of his suit pants, and frowned. McKenna looked down at the display, it was an unfamiliar number.

If Daisy was with them then he would've ignored the call but, since he was a very over-protective daddy, Jed, as McKenna expected him to, answered the call. She couldn't hear the caller's words but she saw the color leach from his face and when he lowered her to the floor, he shook his head, indicating that this had nothing to do with their daughter. But she knew that it was still bad news, something had happened.

Jed ended the call and stared at his phone for a minute before running a hand through his hair. He looked at her and she could see the panic flickering in his eyes. "Damn my gut for being right. Shit!!"

"What's wrong?" McKenna demanded.

Jed gripped the bridge of his nose with his thumb and forefinger. "The beautiful bride, still in my mother's fabulous gown, is sitting in a jail cell downtown."

Now that was one hell of a way to start your honeymoon. McKenna watched as Jed walked to the table to get his car keys, wallet, and room card. Then she slipped her feet back into her shoes and slid her fingers into her husband's, her bad boy's, her good man's, waiting hand.

Together they could face anything. And everything.

The End

The Pytheon Security Series

Get every book in the Pytheon Security series – available now!

Book 1: *Claimed by the Warrior*
Jed Hamilton's story

Book 2: *His Toughest Call*
Seth Halcott's story

Book 3: *In the Line of Fire*
Jett Smith-Jones' story
Seth Halcott's story

About the Author

Joss Wood's passion for putting black letters on a white screen is only matched by her love of books and travelling (especially to the wild places of Southern Africa) and, possibly, by her hatred of ironing and making school lunches.

After juggling a career in business lobbying and economic development with writing, and somehow managing to produce sixteen books, Joss now spends her days creating contemporary fairy tales. She lives in Kwazulu-Natal, South Africa with her husband and two children surrounded by family, friends, animals and a ridiculous amount of reading material.

Thank you for reading

Claimed by the Warrior

If you enjoyed this book, you can find more from all our great authors at TulePublishing.com, or from your favorite online retailer.

Made in the USA
Columbia, SC
16 October 2018